KU-484-012

Dear reader,

NATE, THIS IS **THE FIFTH TIME** I'VE BORROWED THAT BOOK!

I KNOW!

LIBRARY

I CAN'T GET ENOUGH OF *MAX & THE MIDKNIGHTS: BATTLE OF THE BODKINS!*

STORY BEGINS WITH IN KNIGHT SCHOOL...

KLONG CLONG CLANG KLANG

DOOF! **WHUMP!**

BUT IS SHE GOOD ENOUGH?

SURE SHE IS! LOOK AT ALL THE AMAZING STUFF SHE DID IN BOOK **ONE**!

BUT THERE ARE **NEW** CHALLENGES THIS TIME!

NEW VILLAINS...

NEW BEASTS...

AND *BODKINS!*

WHAT **ARE** BODKINS?

YOU'LL KNOW THEM WHEN YOU SEE THEM!

OR **WILL** YOU?

HAPPY READING!!

Nate Wright

MAX
& the Midknights

BATTLE of the BODKINS

Lincoln Peirce

MACMILLAN CHILDREN'S BOOKS

First published 2020 in the US by Delacorte Press
an imprint of Random House Children's Books,
a division of Penguin Random House LLC, New York

This edition published 2021 in the UK by Macmillan Children's Books
an imprint of Pan Macmillan
The Smithson, 6 Briset Street, London EC1M 5NR
EU representative: Macmillan Publishers Ireland Limited,
Mallard Lodge, Lansdowne Village, Dublin 4
Associated companies throughout the world
www.panmacmillan.com

ISBN 978-1-5290-2928-4

1 3 5 7 9 8 6 4 2

A CIP catalogue record for this book is available from the British Library.

Printed and bound by CPI Group (UK) Ltd, Croydon CR0 4YY

For friends everywhere

I think Sir Brickbat hates me.

We've been practising our sword-fighting skills for three hours now, and he's been yelling the whole time – mostly at yours truly. The question is:

WHY??

I mean, it's not like I'm the worst one here. Some of these kids can't tell a sword from a salami. But whenever our fearless leader wants to air out his tonsils . . .

...I'M HIS FAVOURITE TARGET!

HOLD YOUR HANDS HIGHER!

OR... ✳CHUCKLE!✳... ARE YOU TOO TIRED?

"I'm not tired," I mumble.
"Is that so?" he snorts.

THEN THERE'S NO EXCUSE FOR YOUR **POOR TECHNIQUE**!

What? My technique's just fine. Our INSTRUCTOR'S the problem. Not that I'd ever say that out loud. At KSB – Knight School of Byjovia – the most important lesson isn't sword fighting or archery. It's keeping your eyes open . . .

...AND YOUR MOUTH **SHUT**!

HERE'S AN IDEA!...

SEDGEWICK WILL SHOW YOU HOW IT'S DONE!

Ugh. Couldn't someone ELSE show me how it's done?

Of all the first years in the class, Sedgewick's the most annoying. It's not that he's a bad student. Just the opposite. He's good. REALLY good.

THAT'S WHAT'S SO **OBNOXIOUS** ABOUT HIM!

GO **EASY**, SEDGEWICK!

REMEMBER, SHE'S ONLY A **GIRL**!

"ONLY A GIRL"?

I feel my cheeks burning as Sir Brickbat's words hang in the air. I could tell he didn't like me, and now I know why. He thinks only BOYS should be knights. If it were up to him, I wouldn't even BE here.

HEY, FORGET THAT STUFF ABOUT GOING EASY!

GIVE ME YOUR BEST!

AAANND... DUEL!

CLANG KLONG

KLANG

CLONG

KLANG CLANG

Just so you know, we're not using real weapons. These are training swords. They're made of steel, but the blades have rounded edges so nobody accidentally loses an arm. It's a safety thing. But safe or not, it still doesn't feel very good to get whacked by a big hunk of metal.

Even if I DID need any help, I wouldn't take it. I can't let everybody think I'm not knight material. I drag myself off the ground, ready for "Max vs. Sedgewick – Round Two".

"Are you serious?" I blurt out. So much for the whole "keep your mouth shut" thing.

"Oh, I'm serious," he growls. "But are YOU?"

OOF!

Welcome to another day in paradise. Pretty glamorous, huh? I figured training to become a knight would be a lot of work...

...BUT NOT **THIS** KIND OF WORK!

Knight School wasn't always such a drag. Actually, when I enrolled here only a month ago, it was GREAT. Ol' Brickbutt wasn't our teacher back then.

SIR GADABOUT WAS IN CHARGE!

Gadabout used to be the commander of the Royal Guard. The guy's a legend. He's as old as these rocks, and twice as tough.

But you know the best thing about him?

HE'S AN AWESOME TEACHER!

— 7 —

OR HE **WAS**. WE'D HAD MAYBE SIX OR SEVEN DAYS OF CLASSES WHEN A SPECIAL VISITOR ARRIVED AT THE SCHOOL.

KING **CONRAD!**

HE AND GADABOUT SPOKE PRIVATELY. THE VERY NEXT DAY, GADABOUT WAS GONE!

THAT'S WHEN **THIS** CLOWN SHOWED UP TO TAKE OVER.

SINCE THEN, KSB HAS BEEN PRETTY ROCKY.

WHUMP!

ROCKY! GET IT?

MAX!

If you don't know who Millie is, I'll keep this short: she's one of my best friends, and she's a Midknight. Wondering who the Midknights are?

"Besides getting some honkin' blisters on my hands? Not much," I tell her. "Just doing some heavy lifting for the world's worst sword fighting teacher."

"Want some help?" Millie asks.

"Sure, I'd LOVE some," I answer.

Did I forget to mention that Millie has magical powers? That's sort of an important detail.

Obvious fact of the day: Mumblin is a wizard. And not some average, everyday wizard, either.

HE WAS ONCE BYJOVIA'S **ROYAL MAGICIAN!**

That was way back in the day, though. By the time Millie and I met him, he was a bit of a mess.

But here's the twist: the old guy wasn't completely washed up after all. When the chips were down, he delivered some pretty cool magic. And he's definitely doing a great job of showing Millie the ropes.

"Must be nice," I say with a sigh.

"What?"

AREN'T YOU SUPPOSED TO BE MOVING **ROCKS**?

ROCKS... ROCKS... HMM...

! !

OH, YOU MEAN **THESE** ROCKS?

URK!... GLNK!

HE'S SPEECHLESS!

AN ADDED BONUS!

NOW WE CAN DO SOMETHING **FUN**!

MORE FUN THAN PRANKING SIR BRICKBAT?

LET'S SEE WHAT KEVYN IS UP TO!

"Great idea!" Kevyn's a Midknight, just like me and Millie.
He's the first person I met when I came to Byjovia.

...AND HE ALSO HAPPENS TO BE A TOTAL **GENIUS!**

SUPER! LET'S GO!

Sir Brickbat is staring slack-jawed at our stone skyscraper as we leave the training yard and make our way through the busy streets.

GREETINGS, SIR MAX!

BLESS YOU, SIR MAX!

ER...HI.

"Do you ever get tired of people thanking you for saving Byjovia?" Millie asks.

I try to deflect the question. "We ALL saved Byjovia."

"The rest of us helped, it's true," she concedes.

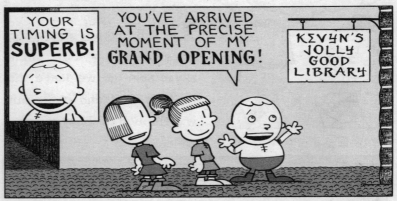

"A library! Kevyn, that's wonderful!" Millie exclaims.

"Yeah, absolutely!" I add.

My eyes widen when I see the cover. "Hey! That's US!"

Kevyn beams. "Yes! It's the entire story of our thrilling adventure, commencing with the auspicious day we met and concluding with King Conrad's triumphant return to the throne!"

Millie flips through the pages, her eyes shining. "Kevyn, it's BEAUTIFUL! I love all the drawings!"

"I say, this is smashing!" Kevyn declares as Simon hops off his horse. "All four Midknights together again!"

Simon gets a hearty handshake from Kevyn and a hug from Millie. Then he walks over to me. "Hi, Max."

To be honest, I wasn't sure how I felt until just now. But seeing Simon right here in front of me, I have no doubts.

"I was never mad at you, Simon," I tell him, and I mean every word. "I was just . . . surprised."

He nods. "Yeah, I was surprised, too, when it happened. But it makes sense now."

"Then explain it to me," I say.

"If you decided to bail because of Sir Brickbat," I tell him, "I totally get it."

Huh? That's not the answer I was expecting, but let's see where he's going with this.

"Last week, after KSB was over for the day, I was walking home," Simon begins.

I STOPPED ON THE WAY TO VISIT NOLAN...

...AND HE DEFINITELY HAD HIS HANDS FULL!

FYI: Nolan is Kevyn's dad, and he owns a stable. Kevyn used to be his apprentice, until he decided he'd rather write books than shovel manure.

GOOD CAREER MOVE BY KEVYN.

ONE HORSE WAS OUT OF CONTROL—BUCKING AND STOMPING!

SUDDENLY, SHE BROKE OUT OF THE PADDOCK!

I MANAGED TO KEEP HER FROM RUNNING WILD IN THE STREETS.

THEN I TALKED TO HER — TO CALM HER DOWN — AND WALKED HER BACK TO THE BARN.

"But HOW?" I ask in amazement. "You don't know anything about horses!"

...DO YOU?

NO! IT WAS JUST LUCK!

BUT NOLAN THOUGHT THERE WAS MORE TO IT.

PERHAPS ONE PERSON IN A **THOUSAND** COULD HAVE HANDLED THIS ANIMAL!

MY BOY, YOU HAVE A **GIFT!**

"After that, I started dropping by the stable every day," Simon continues. "And I LOVED it."

"More than you loved Knight School?" I wonder.

He smiles. "Max, what I liked the most about KSB was hanging out with YOU the whole time."

THE REST OF IT WAS SORT OF... **BORING.**

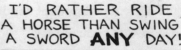

I'D RATHER RIDE A HORSE THAN SWING A SWORD **ANY** DAY!

"Why didn't you just TELL me that?" I yelp.

"I guess I felt guilty," he says with a shrug. "I figured you'd think I was letting you down."

AFTER ALL, WE SAID WE WERE GONNA BECOME KNIGHTS **TOGETHER**!

"I know . . . but we'll always be Midknights, right?" I remind him.

... AND EVERY BAND OF KNIGHTS NEEDS A GOOD HORSEMAN!

WELL SAID, MAX!

I SAY! I'VE JUST REALIZED SOMETHING!

"This development lends a certain SYMMETRY to our group, don't you agree?"

WHAT'S "SYMMETRY"?

I THINK HE MAKES UP WORDS JUST TO MESS WITH US.

WHAT I MEAN IS, **EACH** OF US IS UNUSUALLY **PASSIONATE** ABOUT SOMETHING!

FOR ME, IT'S LITERATURE...

FOR MILLIE, IT'S MAGIC...

FOR SIMON, IT'S HORSES...

...AND FOR **YOU**, MAX, IT'S OBVIOUSLY BEING A KNIGHT!

YEAH, YOU'RE A **NATURAL**!

RIGHT. I'M A NATURAL.

Am I, though? I nod in agreement, but there's not a whole lot of mojo behind it. In the darkest corners of my brain, there's a question lurking – and I don't have an answer.

WHAT IF I'M A **LOUSY KNIGHT**?

Seriously. Before I started Knight School, that never even crossed my mind. I just assumed I'd be top of the class because – sorry to sound braggy – I had a lot of experience.

News flash: it hasn't worked out that way. Sure, some of the students at KSB are about as knightly as a ham sandwich, but what does that make ME? Look at that fiasco during practice earlier.

"Just some stuck-up kid from Knight School," I hiss through gritted teeth.

"You call that stuck-up?" Millie exclaims as Sedgewick disappears around a corner. "He seemed NICE!"

"Precisely what is it about this chap you find so distasteful, Max?" Kevyn asks.

I try to explain. "He's ... well ... he always ... it's just that ..."

That's my uncle Budrick, Byjovia's royal troubadour. Notice I didn't say he's a GOOD troubadour. The guy sings like a frog with a mouth full of marbles.

THISTLE CLUNK PANCAAAAKE!

THANK YOU!

I'LL NOW PASS THE HAT!

DONATIONS GRATEFULLY ACCEPTED!

Lucky for us, King Conrad gave him a job after we helped save Byjovia. As the royal troubadour, Uncle Budrick performs regular shows in the palace. But he still likes to play in public for extra money.

HOW'D YOU DO?

SOMEBODY STOLE MY HAT.

OOH!

MAYBE I CAN HELP WITH A LITTLE *MAGIC!*

"By making him a better singer?" I ask hopefully.

Millie shakes her head. "No, I mean maybe I can replace his hat. I've been practising a new spell."

✳AHEM!✳
Eagle's screech and lion's roar...

"He only needed ONE hat," Simon points out. "Why'd you give him SIX?"

"I wasn't trying to," Millie says, examining her wand. "Maybe I mixed in a duplicating charm by mistake."

"No worries," Uncle Budrick chirps.

I **LIKE** HAVING A FEW EXTRAS!

EXTRAS!! GREAT SCOTT!

"Millie, could you work the same spell on my book?" Kevyn asks breathlessly. "Then my library would have multiple copies!"

"I can try," she tells him. "But first, put the book down and step back."

I DON'T WANT TO DUPLICATE **YOU** AS WELL!

BZZT!

YOWZA! IT **WORKED**!

"FABULOUS, Millie!" Kevyn shouts, dancing around the stack of books. "Each one is an exact replica of the original!"

WAIT A SEC...

THIS ONE'S NOT AN EXACT REPLICA!

LOOK AT THE COVER!

SEE? THE FACES ARE DIFFERENT!

"What about INSIDE the book?" Uncle Budrick asks. I flip it open to check.

HUH.

ALL THE PAGES ARE BLACK!

"How very odd," Kevyn remarks. "The other copies are fine. Only THIS one stands out."

Simon frowns. "But why? What does it mean?"

"Nothing," Millie chimes in. "Just an accident. Stuff like this happens to beginner magicians all the time."

"Work?" I repeat. "Simon, you have a job?"

He's beaming. "Nolan's taken me on as an apprentice."

I feel a twinge of envy as Simon rides off. Hanging around with Nolan all day sounds more fun than getting chewed out by Sir Brickbat. Actually, LOTS of stuff is more fun than that.

Ooh, NOW we're talkin'. Royal receptions are always good. I could do without all the bowing and curtseying, but the food is . . . well, you know. Fit for a king.

We say our goodbyes to Kevyn and head for the castle. There are guards at the gate, but they wave us through.

THANKS, GUYS!

BEING THE ROYAL TROUBADOUR HAS ITS ADVANTAGES!

He's right. Not many people can just stroll into the palace and crash one of the king's fancy-pants parties. And how many girls my age can say they knew the king when he was only a kid?

LONG STORY. READ KEVYN'S BOOK.

BUDRICK! MAX! COME IN!

UH...HOW COME YOU'RE DRESSED LIKE A PARADE FLOAT?

I WISH I WASN'T. I FEEL LIKE A TWIT.

...BUT IT'S TRADITIONAL FOR THE KING TO DRESS FORMALLY WHEN MEETING ANOTHER MONARCH.

"Another monarch?" I echo. "You mean a king?"

"A queen, in this case," Conrad answers. "Nerelia, from the land of Tresk."

Uncle Budrick perks up. "Ah! A distinguished visitor!"

Good call. The last thing this party needs is Uncle Budrick trying to find a rhyme for "Nerelia". Just then there's a blare of trumpets. The reception is starting.

I'm hoping for a quick handshake followed immediately by an all-you-can-eat buffet, but no such luck.

Rats. Hang in there, stomach. This is gonna take a while.

"Uh . . . is that bad?" the king asks.

"On my word, Queen Nerelia, there is no evil in the halls of this castle!" Conrad assures her.

But she's not listening. She stands still as a statue, staring intently at the tip of the sceptre. I see its pale gleam reflected in her eyes. After several long moments, she speaks.

"The crystal is never wrong. Trust me, there is a threat among us – here, in this very room!"

King Conrad looks stunned. "But . . . where?"

3

Uh . . . WHAT?! Some random crystal lights up like a candle, and suddenly I'M the skunk at the picnic? That's ridiculous. This lady's sceptre must be broken.

I'M NO THREAT! HONEST!

I SEE THAT NOW, MY DEAR GIRL...

...AND I HOPE YOU'LL FORGIVE ME FOR ALARMING YOU!

She smiles – a FRIENDLY smile, not one of those Sir Brickbat specials – and I breathe a little easier. As queens go, I'm guessing Nerelia is one of the good ones.

"I made a mistake," she explains. "I thought the crystal was reacting to YOU."

BUT I BELIEVE WHAT YOU'RE **CARRYING** IS THE CULPRIT!

!

I'd almost forgotten about it: the funky copy of Kevyn's book tucked under my arm.

"May I see it, please?" the queen asks, and I hand it to her.

She shuffles to the centre of the throne room and places the book on the floor. Then she waves the sceptre over it. Nothing happens that I can see, but . . .

SNIFF! I **SMELL** SOMETHING!

SORRY. I HAD CHILLI FOR LUNCH.

IT'S NOT **YOU**, UNCLE BUDRICK! IT'S THE **BOOK!**

Imagine all the nastiest stuff you can think of – dead fish, cat pee, artichoke dip – and then set it on fire. That's what the book smells like. But I'm not sure this thing really IS a book. It's starting to twitch and tremble. It seems ALIVE.

The book's black pages are breaking free of the binding and rising into the air like windblown leaves. Except leaves aren't this organized. They hover for a moment and then shuffle together to form . . . well, see for yourself.

And then it's over. The foul smell disappears. The pages fall apart and flutter harmlessly to the floor.

"I'm not sure I can explain it," Queen Nerelia answers, "but the crystal clearly sensed the presence of evil."

"So . . . a book can be evil?" I ask.

"It can if it's a diet book," Uncle Budrick mutters.

"Let's take it to Mumblin," I suggest. "Maybe he can tell us more about it."

"A splendid idea, Max," King Conrad agrees.

BUDRICK, PLEASE ENTERTAIN OUR GUEST WHILE MAX AND I ARE GONE.

YES, YOUR HIGHNESS!

M'LADY, HERE'S A LI'L DITTY CALLED "I'M JUST A KNIGHT WHOSE ARMOUR IS TOO TIGHT"!

UH... OKAY.

PLINK!

EACH DAY I DRESS IN STAINLESS STEEL!... THOSE IRON UNDIES MAKE ME SQUEAL!...

TWANG

TWONG

Poor Queen Nerelia. I don't have the heart to tell her that this song includes a twenty-minute lute solo. Anyway, I gather up all the pages while the king changes out of his monkey suit. Five minutes later, we're on our way to see Mumblin.

"It's for RETIRED people," I remind him. "But Mumblin's UNRETIRED, remember?"

"I imagine he enjoys the company," Conrad says.

"Ah, yes, the BOOK!" Mumblin declares, taking it from me. "Millie mentioned it. I'm curious to have a closer look."

"When Millie told you about it, all she'd seen was the COVER," I tell him. "A lot more has happened since then."

"Evidently," the old wizard says as he notices the rumpled pages I jammed back into the binding. "Please elaborate."

As we walk along the path to Mumblin's cottage, Conrad and I describe the scene in the throne room, including the words we heard coming from that freaky giant face.

Mumblin pulls a magnifying glass from his robes and squints through the lens at the pitch-black pages. To me, it's just a book. But when you're a super-powerful wizard, you can probably see stuff the rest of us can't.

Wait, THAT'S the big reveal? Excuse me while I yawn. I've seen COIN FLIPS that were more dramatic.

"What I mean," Mumblin continues, noticing my epic eyeroll, "is that it's DISGUISED as a book. But as the events in the throne room proved, it's something else entirely."

Okay, I'll bite. "What's a bodkin?"

"A copy," Mumblin answers. "A twin. This book is the bodkin to Kevyn's original."

"Not a REAL twin, though," I interrupt. "I could see right away it was different."

"Yes, bodkins have never learned to become TRULY identical copies," Mumblin explains.

Mumblin nods. "They certainly can be."

I DON'T GET IT.

NEITHER DO **I**! WHO **ARE** THESE BODKINS? WHERE DO THEY **COME** FROM?

"It is said that they live in a secret land – a shadow world that cannot be found on any map," Mumblin states.

HOW AND WHY THEY ENDED UP THERE, I CANNOT SAY.

I CAN!

It's Seymour, and he's carrying a book – I HOPE it's just a book – the size of a pizza box.

ARE YOU GOING TO MAKE ME A PINEAPPLE AGAIN?

SOUNDS FUN! MAYBE LATER!

BUT **FIRST**, I'M GOING TO READ YOU THE **STORY**...

In the olden days of Byjovia, there lived a prince named Torin. He had wealth and power, but was he grateful for his blessings? No, he was selfish and vain, with a vile temper that made him feared and despised throughout the kingdom.

One day, Torin was visited by his fairy dogmother...

UH... SHOULDN'T THAT BE **GODMOTHER?**

YES, BUT THERE'S NO WAY TO CORRECT TYPOS IN THE MIDDLE AGES.

OKAY.

...who said to him, "If you are to one day be king, you must become a better man. Let me help you."

Each day, the fairy dogmother removed one of Torin's many demons and stored them in a magical  bottle where they could do no harm. And each day Torin grew wiser and kinder, until finally he was worthy of being king.

But the night before he was to be crowned, Torin knocked the bottle from its shelf. It shattered, releasing the demons from their captivity.

 Lo and behold, the demons bonded together and in appearance became the very image of Torin himself! "Look upon me," he commanded. "I am called Boris."

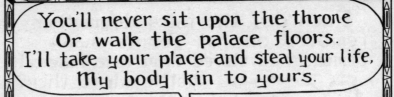

You'll never sit upon the throne
Or walk the palace floors.
I'll take your place and steal your life,
My body kin to yours.

"MY **BODY KIN** TO YOURS"! THAT'S WHY THEY'RE CALLED **BODKINS**, RIGHT?

PRECISELY!

THEN WHAT HAPPENED?

Boris overpowered Torin and imprisoned him in a cave. Then he became king in the prince's place, ruling Byjovia with threats and cruelty.

But Torin escaped and returned to face the bodkin.

"Which of them is the imposter?" the people cried. "They are identical!"

"Aha! I'll bet they WEREN'T identical, though, were they?" I shout. "Mumblin said there's always something ODD about bodkins!"

"And so there was in this case," Seymour confirms.

ACCORDING TO THE STORY, BORIS HAD NO **FINGERNAILS!**

THAT SOUNDS KINDA GREAT, ACTUALLY. ONE LESS THING TO KEEP CLEAN.

THE PEOPLE SEIZED THE BODKIN AND DEMANDED HE BE PUNISHED.

Prince Torin summoned the fairy dogmother. He asked her to create a captive realm deep in the forest from which Boris couldn't escape.

Before he was taken away, Boris drew close to Torin and whispered in his ear. Then he left Byjovia, never to return.

The End

"No, they haven't," Conrad says softly.

Huh? No offence, big fella, but . . . says who?

"Every member of Byjovia's royal line of succession has learned those words," Conrad goes on. "They've been passed down through generations of kings and queens."

"Can you tell us the words, Your Highness?" Mumblin asks.

You've banished me I know not where,
But others soon will join me there.
And come the day when we break free,
A mighty army we shall be.

"I say, this chap had a knack for reciting rather ominous poetry," Seymour observes.

"If a bunch of bodkins are forming an army," I exclaim, "we need to get ready NOW! Before it's too late!"

Mumblin's face is clouded with worry as he strokes his beard. "I'm afraid you don't understand, Max."

"What are you saying, old friend?" Conrad's voice is deadly serious. "Is Byjovia in danger?"

"I believe it is, Your Majesty," Mumblin replies.

THIS **BOOK** YOU AND MAX BROUGHT ME **PROVES** IT!

"How so?" the king demands.

"The book is a bodkin," Mumblin reminds us. "If it found a way into our world . . ."

"Enough," Conrad commands, sounding royally peeved. "What shall we do about the bodkins? Warn the people?"

Mumblin shakes his head. "That would only panic them."

GIVE ME TIME TO EXAMINE THE BOOK FURTHER!

MEANWHILE, LET'S ALL JUST BEHAVE NORMALLY!

EASY FOR **YOU** TO SAY! **YOU'RE** NOT A **DANISH!**

TRUE. I'M 60% IRISH, 40% SCOTTISH, AND 10% TASMANIAN!

WAIT A MINUTE! THAT'S **110%!**

I COME FROM A LARGE FAMILY.

GOODNIGHT, MUMBLIN. WE'LL SPEAK TOMORROW.

Conrad and I leave for the castle. There's not a sound in the evening air. Guess it's my job to break the silence.

"Poor Seymour. I'll bet it's not much fun being a cinnamon roll." There's item one on the "Things You Never Thought You'd Say" list.

The king chuckles. "I'm sure Mumblin will change him back to a wizard before he turns stale."

Stale. Get it? Not great, but give the guy a break. He's a monarch, not a stand-up comedian.

YOUR HIGHNESS... HOW MUCH DID YOU KNOW ABOUT BODKINS BEFORE TONIGHT?

A faraway look crosses Conrad's face. "When I was a boy, my parents told me many stories. Some may have been more legend than truth. But I believed them."

"What did they say?"

"That each of us has a bodkin."

IN THE SHADOW LAND, THERE'S A BODKIN FOR EVERY MAN, WOMAN, AND CHILD IN BYJOVIA!

AND THEY ALL LOOK EXACTLY LIKE **US!**

"So if you've got a humongous zit on your butt," I ask . . .

"Yes," the king agrees. "But what really concerns me is Mumblin's prediction about the bodkins' plans."

The king kneels down next to me. "You've just confirmed that Mumblin was right when he advised us against warning people," he whispers. "Can't you see what that would mean?"

WE'D ALL START TO SEE BODKINS AROUND EVERY CORNER!

...AS **YOU** JUST DID.

I feel my cheeks burning. I guess maybe I did go a little overboard there.

"For now, let's assume that there AREN'T any bodkins in Byjovia," the king suggests as we reach the castle and pass through the main gate.

I'D MUCH RATHER BELIEVE THE **BEST** ABOUT A PERSON THAN SUSPECT THE **WORST**!

Queen Nerelia looks limper than a week-old salad. Conrad shows her to the guest quarters, while I drag Uncle Budrick from the throne room. But he's not ready to pack it in.

He sprays – er, PLAYS it for me as we walk home. Thank goodness our cottage is only two verses away. We share a barely edible supper, and then I go straight to bed.

Maybe it's all the bodkins talk, or maybe it's the acid reflux from Uncle Budrick's courgette casserole. Whatever's to blame, I'm restless. And when I'm restless . . .

First the good news: this isn't one of those dreams where I'm running around in my underwear while everyone else is fully clothed. Phew.

Now the bad: Sir Brickbat's in the very first scene, which officially moves us into nightmare territory.

THERE'S NO PATH, NO LANDMARKS.

I'M **LOST**.

I NOTICE SOMETHING ON THE GROUND.

NERELIA'S SCEPTRE!

!

AH! IT'S **MAX**! THE GIRL WHO WANTS TO BE A **KNIGHT**!

BUT TELL ME: WHAT KIND OF KNIGHT GETS **LOST** IN THE **FOREST**?

GIVE UP! IT'S CLEAR YOU DON'T HAVE WHAT IT **TAKES**!

YOU'LL **NEVER** BE A KNIGHT! **NEVER!**

SUDDENLY I HEAR A FAMILIAR VOICE.

THIS WAY, MAX!

THAT'S **MILLIE!**

I COME TO A CLEARING, AND THERE'S MILLIE, STANDING BESIDE A GIGANTIC TREE.

COME HERE, MAX. THERE'S SOMEONE I'D LIKE YOU TO MEET.

A FIGURE APPEARS, DRIFTING OUT OF THE TRUNK LIKE A **GHOST**.

HELLO, MAX.

WHAT'S WRONG?

DON'T YOU **RECOGNIZE** ME?

That's when I wake up, sweating buckets. Nothing like a bodkin dream to ruin a good night's sleep.

I try to shut my eyes again, but I'm too rattled. A few hours of tossing and turning later, it's morning.

You think sleepwalking is strange? Try living with a sleep-SINGER. I do my best to ignore Uncle Budrick's vocal stylings as I eat a quick breakfast. Then I take off with Mumblin's words from yesterday ringing in my ears:

"BEHAVE NORMALLY."

Would I rather be preparing for a bodkin invasion? Sure. But instead, I'm going to stick to my routine, go to KSB . . .

. . . AND SAY HI TO **KEVYN** ALONG THE WAY!

KEVYN! WHAT'S UP?

HELLO!

NON-FICTION

Hello? That's IT? Pretty vanilla by his usual standards. I'm used to his more Kevyn-ish greetings, like . . .

"SALUTATIONS!"

"GOOD MORROW!"

"HAIL-FELLOW-WELL-MET!"

"ALOHA!"

No time to worry about that now, though. I hustle towards the training yard. The last thing I need is Sir Brickbat throwing a hairy fit because . . .

"But . . . nobody told me that yesterday!" I protest.

Sir Brickbat snickers. "How very strange! None of the BOYS forgot about this morning's competition!"

"Very well, then," Sir Brickbat grumbles.

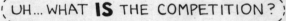

LET THE COMPETITION BEGIN!

UH... WHAT **IS** THE COMPETITION?

"Orienteering," Sedgewick answers. "Knights need to know where they're going, even without a map to guide them."

THE OBJECT IS TO FIND OUR WAY HOME FROM THE MIDDLE OF **NOWHERE!**

"These clouds will carry your teams to an unknown location," Sir Brickbat announces. "The first team to return to the training ground will be declared the winner."

START CLIMBING!

He doesn't have to tell us twice. Sedgewick and I scramble up the rope ladder, and in a matter of seconds we've got our heads in the clouds – literally.

Our cloud gradually drifts away from the others, until they're all out of sight. Sedgewick cranes his neck over one fluffy edge, staring at the landscape far below.

"Hey," I ask him. "Why'd you pick me as a partner?"

"I want to win," he answers matter-of-factly. "And you're the best student in the class."

Wait, Knighty McKnight is calling ME the best? I've been feeling like the class idiot.

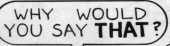

WHY WOULD YOU SAY **THAT**?

WE DON'T EVEN **LIKE** EACH OTHER!

He looks surprised. "Speak for yourself. I don't dislike anyone – except Sir Brickbat, of course."

What? I thought Sedgewick LOVED ol' Brickbrain.

"But if you've decided you don't like ME for some reason," he continues . . .

...THAT'S **YOUR** BUSINESS!

Great. Now I feel GUILTY. Do we really have to talk about feelings and all that junk?

CAN'T WE JUST HAVE THE OCCASIONAL SWORD FIGHT AND LEAVE IT AT THAT?

HEY! WE'RE **LANDING**!

He's right. No need for a ladder this time. Our cloud descends into a grove of trees and lands gently on the forest floor. Sedgewick and I jump down.

There's no doubt about it: that's the tree I saw in my nightmare. My heart starts hammering in my chest. I don't have a good feeling about this.

"We may need to defend ourselves," I whisper, keeping my eyes on the tree. "So be ready. Okay, Sedgewick?"

5

Where'd he go? He was right behind me.

"SEDGEWICK?" I wait for an answer. Crickets.

Well, this stinks. Just two minutes after our friendly neighbourhood cloud drops us in some random field . . .

"Where WERE you?" I demand, sounding more like a panicky chipmunk than a future knight. "I turned around and you were GONE!"

He shrugs. "I've been right here the whole time."

I hesitate. Do I really want to tell Sedgewick I saw this place in my SLEEP? He'll think I've lost it.

"It . . . er . . . seems familiar, that's all," I say finally.

"Why don't we look around a bit?" Sedgewick suggests.

That's when I see it – right there on Sedgewick's cheek.

Let's be clear about one thing:
I have NOT spent a lot of time
looking at Sedgewick's face. But
I'm good at noticing stuff, and I'm pretty sure – no, I'm
POSITIVE – that there wasn't a freckle on his cheek before.

Hmm. Remember what Mumblin said about bodkins?

And make no mistake: an instant freckle is definitely odd.
The question is, does it mean what I THINK it means?

I know, I know – it's a wild idea. But what if it's NOT? I was
staring at the tree, not paying attention to Sedgewick.

"Just getting something out of my knapsack," I answer as casually as I can.

"Like a WEAPON?" Sedgewick counters. His voice is cold.

"I told you before, we may need to defend ourselves," I remind him. I feel for the hilt of my dagger inside the bag and grip it tight.

I pull my blade from the knapsack. "I can fight my own battles, thanks."

"Against whatever lives in that tree?" he growls.

"Same difference," I say. "I know what you are."

YOU'RE A **BODKIN.**

His mouth twitches into an ugly smirk. For the first time, he looks less than human. "And you're a clever girl," he hisses. "But that's no surprise to me. You see, I know everything Sedgewick knows . . ."

CLONG!

... INCLUDING HOW TO **BEAT** YOU!

Game on, people. Except this isn't a game, and these aren't sparring swords. One wrong move, and I could get sliced up like a loaf of bread.

SLICED BREAD! SOMEONE SHOULD **INVENT** THAT!

SURRENDER, GIRL, OR I'LL CUT YOUR THROAT!

CLANG CLANG CLANG

The bodkin glares at me for a long moment. Then he rises slowly to his feet. "Not bad," he says.

"Where is he?" I snap. "What have you done with the real Sedgewick?"

There's that creepy grin again. "He's quite safe. He's with US now. You're welcome to join him if you'd like."

"Or what?" the bodkin sneers. "You'll kill me? We both know you don't have the stomach for it."

He's right. Knights are supposed to be able to slay their enemies, but I'm not that ruthless. I feel guilty when I step on an ANT. My arms fall helplessly to my sides as he walks towards the tree . . .

. . . AND DISAPPEARS INTO THE TRUNK!

Wow. But why am I surprised? My dream already showed me that this tree is a gateway to the bodkin world.

... AND SEDGEWICK'S A **PRISONER** THERE!

What do I do? If I walk through the tree, I'll probably get gang-tackled by a gazillion bodkins. But if I just wait around, Sedgewick could be toast.

THERE'S ONLY ONE CHOICE! I'M **GOIN' IN!**

THWOCK!

Uh . . . no, I'm not. At least not until I find out who's using me for target practice.

"But I HAVE to touch the tree!" I protest. "My friend is—"

He places a finger to his lips. "We're not abandoning your friend, Max. But if we want to help him, we must first learn more about what we'll be facing."

"What kind of creatures?"

"They are called Crags," Gadabout replies. "I've never seen them. They're said to be made of stone."

"I think we're safe, then," I say.

Okay, just a wild guess: that's a Crag. And he doesn't seem like the cuddly type.

I don't need to hear it twice. A knight knows a mismatch when she sees one. And the odds are getting worse.

WHAT? We're about to get pounded into the ground like tent stakes, and he's having a SNACK?

Ah! I forgot that Mumblin uses fruit to communicate. He and I once had a long-distance conversation on a banana.

We interrupt this disaster to remind you that this is a man who accidentally turned himself into a pastry. And we're depending on HIM to rescue us.

"Will you grant us another favour?" asks Gadabout. "We must speak to Mumblin right away – IN PERSON."

The little wizard sighs. "Unfortunately, I'm lousy at magical transportation. But I can call you a Cab."

Gadabout nods. "We'd appreciate it."

I've never ridden a griffin before. We climb on to Cab's back and prepare for lift-off.

My review of travelling by griffin: mixed. It's way faster than a cloud, but the seats aren't as comfortable.

I describe the orienteering competition. "What about you?" I ask. "How come YOU were there?"

"I was on a mission for the king," Gadabout says.

"A mission about bodkins?"

He shakes his head. "No . . . something else." That's all he says, though. Before I can find out more, we're landing in front of the royal palace.

They don't look as shocked as I thought they would. Actually, they don't seem surprised at all.

"We've had a similar experience, Max," Mumblin says. "But we didn't just SEE a bodkin . . ."

"You DID?" I can't hide my amazement. "Where is he?"

"It's not a he, Max," the old wizard says gently. "Prepare yourself."

That's when King Conrad turns to one of his soldiers. "Bring the prisoner here," he orders.

The guard moves off to another room. I hear the rattle of chains, followed by the sound of approaching footsteps.

"Are you two out of your minds?" I shout. Kind of a sassy way
to speak to a king and a wizard, but I can't help myself.

MILLIE'S NOT A BODKIN!

YOU'RE MAKING A TERRIBLE MISTAKE!

"I've made many mistakes in my life," Mumblin admits.

"Er . . . sorry," the old wizard says. "My point is, this is NOT one of those mistakes. We are in the presence of a bodkin."

The queen approaches, one hand tightly gripping the shaft of her sceptre. She lowers it, points it at Millie, and . . .

That settles it, all right. The face I thought was Millie's twists into an ugly scowl. "I don't understand," she snarls. "What made you suspect me?"

"You forget, perhaps, that Millie is my apprentice," Mumblin replies. "I saw by the way you held her wand that you were an imposter."

"Where's the REAL Millie?" I demand.

That's more like it. The bodkin slumps against the wall as the magic takes hold. Her eyes turn glassy.

"Let us begin," Mumblin declares.

"Tell us about this . . . Knot," King Conrad

"If I must," hisses the bodkin.

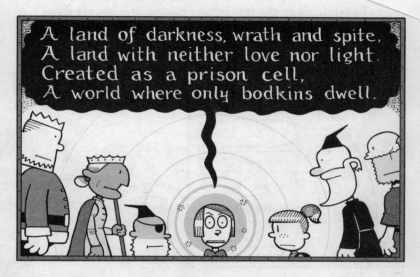

A land of darkness, wrath and spite,
A land with neither love nor light.
Created as a prison cell,
A world where only bodkins dwell.

"Not ONLY bodkins dwell there!" I interrupt.

MILLIE AND SEDGEWICK ARE THERE, **TOO!**

The bodkin nods. "Among others."

"What others?" Mumblin asks sharply.

But this time, the bodkin doesn't respond. It's Nerelia's voice that breaks the silence.

THE **OTHERS** SHE REFERS TO...

...ARE THE **DWARFS OF TRESK!**

"That's correct," the bodkin rasps.

"They've been disappearing from our land for weeks now," Nerelia explains to the rest of us. "But no one knows why."

"The dwarfs of Tresk are peaceful people," Gadabout says.

"But now she can't answer any more questions!" I cry.

"We have learned enough," Mumblin states.

I tear out of the castle like my hair's on fire and dash to the stable. I don't know exactly what the job is . . .

I tell him everything, and right away he's all in – even if it takes him a while to catch on.

Convincing Kevyn to join us might be tough. He's not exactly a natural-born adventurer. But when he hears that Millie's in trouble . . .

When we arrive, everyone's seated in the royal dining room – including Uncle Budrick, Byjovia's biggest buzzkill.

"I believe I understand the bodkins' plan," the magician begins. "But first, I must confirm a suspicion."

"Indeed," she confirms. "The women are musicians and entertainers of the highest order."

"And I'm guessing that it's only the men who've gone missing, yes?" Mumblin adds.

Nerelia looks surprised. "That's right. How did you—?"

"Ah. I understand now," Conrad says, his face grim.

"Their scheme is clear," Mumblin declares. "They're kidnapping the dwarfs and forcing them to produce weapons. Once every bodkin is armed and armoured . . ."

"Okay, so that's THEIR plan," I say.

"Aha!" Simon exclaims. "That's where the Midknights come in, right?"

Mumblin smiles. "Correct. You'll travel to the land of Knot and free the prisoners."

...AND WITH ANY LUCK, YOU'LL FIND A WAY TO **STOP** THE BODKINS ALTOGETHER!

OH, IS **THAT** ALL?

WAIT, DO WE EVEN KNOW WHERE KNOT **IS**?

"Max and I have seen the entrance," answers Gadabout. "A giant tree in the Wandering Woods."

"So what do we do?" I ask.

WALK UP TO THE TREE AND RING THE **DOORBELL**?

WHAT'S A DOORBELL?

I'LL BET THAT TREE WILL BE **CRAWLING** WITH GUARDS!

AND THEY'LL BE ON THE LOOKOUT FOR A RESCUE PARTY!

I notice a sudden gleam in Gadabout's eye. "What if you WEREN'T a rescue party?" he proposes.

WE'RE DWARFS!

DWARFS OF TRESK, TO BE EXACT!

THIS IS HOW YOU'LL GET TO KNOT!

SERIOUSLY? BY LETTING OURSELVES BE KIDNAPPED?

"Exactly! The bodkins will never suspect your TRUE intentions," Gadabout explains.

King Conrad nods in agreement. "They'll think you're metalsmiths, just like the dwarfs they've already captured."

FROM ONE TINY, BEARDED MAN TO ANOTHER: YOU LOOK FABULOUS!

I FEEL LIKE I HAVE A RACCOON ON MY FACE.

THINK I CAN SWAP THIS FOR A HANDLEBAR MOUSTACHE?

"How come YOU guys aren't dwarfs?" I ask the adults. "Aren't you coming to Knot?"

The king shakes his head. "Our place is here in Byjovia. We must protect the realm – and search for any bodkins hiding among our people."

SO...IT'S JUST THE THREE OF US?

...VERSUS A BUTTLOAD OF BODKINS?

NOT QUITE!

SEYMOUR WILL COME WITH YOU TO PROVIDE MAGICAL SUPPORT!

GREAT. WE CAN **BAGPIPE** THEM TO DEATH!

AND **BUDRICK** WILL JOIN YOU AS WELL!

ME?

BUT I'M TOO **BIG** TO BE A DWARF!

Simon chuckles. "This is amazing, Mumblin! When we find Millie, she won't recognize us!"

"Good gravy! I nearly forgot!" the sorcerer cries. He takes Millie's wand from his pocket and hands it to me.

"Bring this to her," he says. I slip the wand inside my boot.

"I, too, have something for you, young lady," Queen Nerelia announces. (BTW: it's weird being called "young lady" when you've got a face full of whiskers.)

"I'd give you a sword," Gadabout tells me, "but carrying a weapon would give away your real identity."

"That's OK," I assure him.

SOON ENOUGH WE'LL BE UP TO OUR **EARS** IN WEAPONS.

WE'RE DWARFS. WE'RE UP TO OUR EARS IN **EVERYTHING**.

GOOD POINT.

King Conrad shakes our hands. "Safe travels, Midknights."

ON BEHALF OF ALL BYJOVIANS, I WISH YOU GOOD FORTUNE!

We follow the long corridor to the castle's front entrance. Cab is waiting there, along with another griffin.

"Where to?"

"Back to where you found us before," I say. All of us climb aboard. Some rescue party. We look like a gang of runaways from Santa's workshop.

"Okay, Midknights," I tell them. "Here we go . . ."

As we soar across the sky on our way to the Wandering Woods, I can't help but feel a little uneasy. And it's not because Seymour keeps quoting gruesome safety facts.

No, what's got me worried is how little we know about where we're going. And for some reason, everyone's expecting ME to lead the way. But I don't have a map.

"Let's make sure we're not spotted," I tell Cab. "Take us down behind that ridge." She nods and starts a descent. Minutes later, we're on the ground.

We jump behind some bushes as two figures emerge from a grove of trees. So THAT'S who set the crystal off.

"I haven't seen the girl before," I whisper. "But the boy is Sedgewick's bodkin."

"Sounds like they were on a dwarf hunt and came up empty," Simon observes.

I nod. "We can fix that. Come on, Midknights . . ."

LET'S GET **CAPTURED!**

♪ HEIGH HO!... ♪

WE'RE JUST A SIMPLE DWARF PARADE AND METAL IS OUR STOCK-IN-TRADE! PLEASE PARDON US IF THIS SOUNDS BOLD: OUR CRAFTSMANSHIP IS SOLID GOLD!

WE MAKE UTENSILS! JEWELLERY! CLOCKS! WE MAKE THE KEYS THAT UNLOCK LOCKS! MOUSETRAPS! DOORKNOBS! SHOVELS! RAKES! WE MAKE 'EM ALL, FOR GOODNESS' SAKES!

METALSMITHS, ARE YOU? THEN YOU'RE JUST THE DWARFS WE'RE LOOKING FOR!

COME WITH US. **NOW!**

- 112 -

Well, THAT was easy. I thought fake Sedgewick would see through my disguise. But this beard must be pretty convincing.

The two bodkins march us over the ridge. There in the clearing, the gateway to Knot looms high above us.

"That's one scary tree," mutters Simon.

"Y'know what would make it LESS scary?" Seymour says.

Three times, Sedgewick's bodkin strikes the tree with the flat of his sword. A leaf flutters down from the branches. Then another. Then . . .

In a roar of wind, we're swept off our feet and sucked into a swirling funnel. Then, just as suddenly, the wind stops and we're back on the ground. But there's no grass, no leaves. We're not in the Wandering Woods any longer.

I can't see a thing, but this FEELS like a tunnel. And sure enough, as I take a few cautious steps forward, I can make out a faint glow in the distance. It's an opening – a door,

or some kind of archway. I push towards it – then THROUGH it – and out into the open. I blink hard and look around.

First impressions? Not great. The streets look like a pigsty and smell like a cesspool. This place is a DUMP. And yet . . .

"They're perfect copies," Simon states. "Except they all look kind of mad."

The forge. That must be where the dwarfs are making

weapons. But what about Millie and Sedgewick? They're not metalsmiths, so I doubt we'll find them there. They've got to be somewhere else.

We proceed single file through the filthy streets. Before long we reach the outskirts of the city and turn on to a rugged path. It's isolated, with no other travellers around – the perfect place to make my escape.

"A what?" he replies. Speaking of distractions, Kevyn's mind seems to have wandered off. WAY off.

"A DISTRACTION," I repeat. "What's going ON with you?"

"Sorry," he mutters. "I'm not thinking straight. I must be too worried about Millie."

Sure. We all are. But can't Kevyn worry and be a genius at the same time? Apparently not. Which means I'll have to pull this off on my own.

I leap from the path and sprint down a muddy hill towards a cluster of fallen trees. With any luck . . .

Slight problem, though:

"I'm surprised that one rejected you," Sedgewick's bodkin sneers. "Swamp worms usually LIKE the taste of dwarf!"

I stand up, wiping the slime off my clothes. "Maybe I was just too TOUGH for him," I snap.

The girl bodkin scoffs. "We'll see how tough you are . . ."

This is it: the forge. It's a grimy, squat building with a gigantic chimney rising at one end. The bodkins escort us along the path to a mammoth iron door marking the entrance.

"Welcome to your new job!" the bogus Sedgewick cackles.

IT STARTS **NOW** AND ENDS WHEN YOU **DIE**!

WAIT! THERE'S SOMETHING I MUST SAY!

THESE AREN'T **DWARFS**!

THEY'RE **KNIGHTS**!

THEY'VE COME TO RESCUE THEIR FRIENDS AND STOP US FROM TAKING OVER THEIR KINGDOM!

My insides curdle like sour milk as I realize what's happening. Of course — it's OBVIOUS. Why didn't I see it sooner?

YOU'RE NOT KEVYN. YOU'RE A **BODKIN**.

"Guilty as charged." He chuckles. "And now, if you and your little sidekick would be so kind . . ."

GIVE ME THE WANDS.

What choice do we have? Two swords are pointing straight at our backs. Reluctantly, I fish Millie's wand from my boot. Seymour hands his over, too.

"Watch closely!" Kevyn's bodkin crows. "You don't have to be a WIZARD to do magic!"

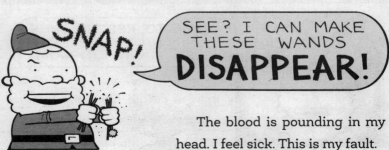

SNAP!

SEE? I CAN MAKE THESE WANDS **DISAPPEAR!**

The blood is pounding in my head. I feel sick. This is my fault.

"I should have known just by LISTENING that you weren't Kevyn," I say as he tosses the splinters aside.

YOU HAVEN'T USED A WORD LONGER THAN TWO SYLLABLES SINCE WE LEFT BYJOVIA!

He smirks. "Yes, I never quite mastered his smarty-farty way of talking."

"And the crystal! I thought it was glowing on account of THOSE two," I continue, pointing at our captors.

...BUT IT WAS REACTING TO **YOU**!

AH! I ALMOST FORGOT ABOUT THE **CRYSTAL**!

I'LL TAKE THAT, TOO.

My cheeks burning with rage, I reach for the chain around my neck. But something's wrong.

The girl bodkin searches me up and down – clothing, boots, cap – and finds nothing but a wad of pocket lint. And a stick of gum. And a marble. And a piece of chalk.

"The creatures in charge of the forge!" fake Sedgewick sneers as he pushes open the giant door. "And once they find out you can't make weapons, you know what they'll do?"

We're in an enormous room. The clang of hammers on steel fills the air. All around, dozens of dwarfs are crafting weapons. Piles of swords, spears and axes cover the floor.

"And that must be an over-bite," murmurs Simon. We stare across the room at a hulking figure, towering over the nearby dwarfs and holding an axe that's twice my size.

WOW. BAD TEETH.

HE SHOULD SEE AN ORTHODONTIST.

GUYS, **CONCENTRATE!**

UNLESS WE BECOME METALSMITHS **RIGHT NOW**, THAT THING WILL EAT US FOR **LUNCH!**

I spot a weary-looking dwarf just a few yards away, shaping an iron rod into a spear tip. I race over to him.

"Please help us," I gasp.

He peers at me. There's suspicion in his eyes. "And why should I?" he croaks. "You are a stranger."

YOU'RE NOT FROM TRESK.

NO... BUT WE'RE **FRIENDS!**

AND... UH... WE DON'T KNOW HOW TO MAKE WEAPONS.

He frowns. "All dwarfs know how to work metal."

"Well, here's the thing," I tell him. "We're not dwarfs."

He gazes at me again, more carefully this time. "Yes," he agrees. "I can see it now. You are not a dwarf."

Clumps of hair drop from my chin to the floor. I whirl around to look at the others. Simon's losing his beard, too. Uncle Budrick is growing like a beanstalk on steroids.

I can answer that: our magical disguises have fizzled out. Which means our chances of blending in with the dwarfs here in the forge . . .

The CRYSTAL! I was sure I'd lost it when I was halfway down that swamp worm's throat . . .

"It was a gift," I explain. "From Nerelia, the queen of Tresk." The dwarf's face lights up, and he drops to one knee. "A friend of Her Majesty's is a friend of mine!" he exclaims.

Gee, do you suppose the overbites have spotted us yet? I somersault out of the way, landing near a pile of gleaming swords. They're all too big for me. I grab one anyway.

Simon leaps to my side and Rovak grabs a spear, but that won't make much difference. More overbites are coming.

"Even if every last dwarf joins the fight, we can't beat these goons," Simon gasps.

I grip my sword tighter. "Maybe not . . ."

Yikes. I forgot that sometimes trying and losing are the same thing. And this might be one of those times.

ZAP! ZIP! ZUP!

"Doing what?" he asks.

"MAGIC!" I shout. "Kevyn's bodkin took your wand! I saw him snap it in half!"

Seymour beams. "That wasn't my wand, Max!"

"Can we focus on something else?" Simon pleads. "Like GETTING OUT OF HERE?"

Translation: we don't have much time to search for Kevyn, Millie and Sedgewick. To find them, we'll need to be sneaky.

See what I mean? We're about as subtle as a marching band. This won't cut it.

"We should split up," I announce as we file out of the forge.

"I completely agree!" Seymour chirps.

Shock of the day: Uncle Budrick steps in. "Max is my niece!" he tells Rovak. "Wherever she goes, I go!"

"That's brave of you," the dwarf declares. "For I am taking her to the Pits of Doom, deep beneath the bodkin palace."

Uncle Budrick's face turns eggshell-white. "Th-the Pits of D-DOOM, you say?"

Rovak nods. "They are guarded by unspeakable terrors."

ULP! ACTUALLY, I THINK I'LL STICK WITH THE DWARFS.

GOOD PLAN.

We say our goodbyes. Uncle Budrick, Seymour and the dwarfs turn east into the hills beyond the forge. Our group heads west.

HERE, I GRABBED SOME DAGGERS FROM THE PILE.

THANKS...

...AND I'M GOING TO REATTACH THE CRYSTAL TO MY CHAIN.

"It would be wise to keep the gem hidden, Max," Rovak advises. "It has value."

"What kind of value?" Simon wonders as I tuck the crystal under my tunic . . .

...AND WHY DID KEVYN'S BODKIN WANT IT SO BADLY?

I CANNOT SAY.

A shiver runs up my back at the mention of fake Kevyn.

"Hey, guys," I say. "What if we meet our own bodkins?"

A grim-faced sentry gives us a major side-eye as we approach. "What is your purpose here?" she barks.

She peers at us suspiciously. "Then why didn't you follow procedure and feed him to the swamp worms?"

Uh-oh. This lady might be on to us. I decide to ramp up my voice to Full Bodkin.

She steps aside, and we continue along the trail.

He's right. But at each one, we manage to bluff our way through. The road climbs to the crest of a hill, and when we reach the top, a jagged tower comes into view.

"There it is," Rovak announces.

"By DROWNING us?" I splutter. "Interesting technique."

"This moat is the only way to breach the castle walls without being seen," he explains.

THE CURRENT WILL CARRY US THROUGH TUNNELS AND INTO THE CATACOMBS!

HOW DO YOU KNOW ALL THIS?

I WAS THE VERY FIRST DWARF TO BE TAKEN FROM TRESK.

"The bodkins brought me to the palace before moving me to the forge. Everything I saw, I did my best to remember."

DID YOU SEE THE PITS OF DOOM?

ALAS, NO.

I'M NOT CERTAIN HOW TO GET THERE FROM HERE.

AHEM!

PITS OF DOOM

THAT'S A GOOD SIGN!

LET'S GO!

PITS OF DOOM

We scurry through a dark passageway that leads to a chamber roughly the size of Conrad's throne room. But that's where the similarities end.

"Those holes in the floor," Simon whispers. "Are they—?"

"Yes." Rovak nods. "Those must be the Pits of Doom."

No wonder I didn't notice them right away. Hovering high above us are three vague shapes. At first, they look like puffs of smoke. But as my eyes adjust, I can see that they're more than that.

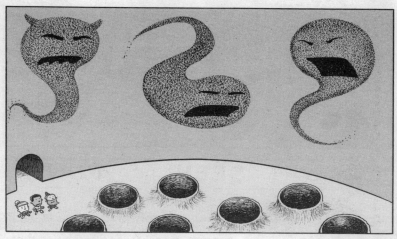

"They look pretty real to ME," Simon mutters.

"What ARE those things, Rovak?" I ask.

"In the stories, they are called formlings," replies the dwarf. "They can become anything. At any time."

THEY'VE **SEEN** US! RUN!

But the only place to go is back the way we came, and I won't do that. Real knights don't retreat – even with a pack of angry formlings closing in on them.

I'M NOT GOIN' DOWN WITHOUT A **FIGHT!**

TRIP!

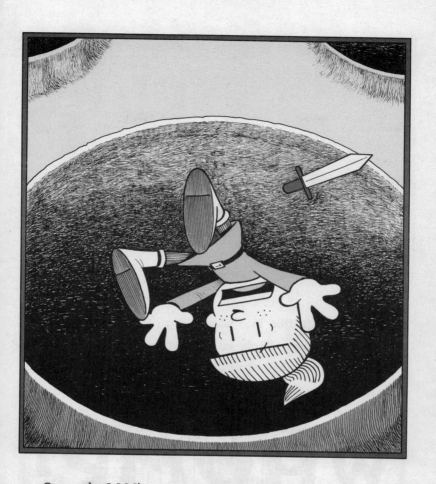

Or maybe I AM!

9

When you belly-flop into something called a Pit of Doom, you're expecting a whole lot of nasty at the bottom – iron spikes, deadly snakes, stuff like that. But for me, it's a pretty soft landing.

WHUMP!

"MAX!" he shouts in disbelief. "What on earth are you doing here?"

"Rescuing YOU," I answer. "At least, that was the plan. Until I made a total mess of it."

I manage a weak smile. Kevyn's trying to cheer me up, but it's not really helping. I blew it. A knight is supposed to save the day . . .

I feel a surge of relief – they're alive! – followed by a wave of guilt. After all, Sedgewick got kidnapped right under my nose. And what about Millie's wand?

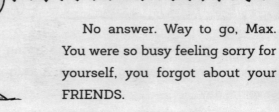

No answer. Way to go, Max. You were so busy feeling sorry for yourself, you forgot about your FRIENDS.

MAYBE THEY GOT AWAY!

THAT'S HIGHLY DOUBTFUL, I'M SORRY TO SAY.

NOTHING ESCAPES THOSE BODKINS!

"Are you talking about the formlings?" I ask. "The shadowy things floating over the pits?"

THOSE ARE **BODKINS**?

INDEED.

THAT'S WHAT THEY LOOK LIKE BEFORE THEY ASSUME THEIR **PERMANENT FORM**!

BEFORE THEY BECOME PEOPLE, YOU MEAN?

OR ANIMALS. OR TREES. BODKINS CAN BE **MANY** THINGS!

DURING MY TIME HERE, I'VE LEARNED QUITE A BIT ABOUT THESE CREATURES!

"Like what?" I ask.

"SHHH!" Kevyn whispers. "Not now."

Two formlings appear at the edge of the pit and then start oozing down the walls. I grasp around on the floor for my blade, but it's too late. They're on us now, shifting from clouds of vapour . . .

. . . into a giant pair of gnarled hands.

I appreciate a firm handshake, but this is ridiculous. We rise through a jumble of tunnels and then up a long stairway into the halls of a gloomy castle. A door swings open, and we're dropped on a floor so cold and hard it makes granite feel like a kitchen sponge.

"But at least we've been REUNITED!" Kevyn reminds me in his usual glass-half-full way. "We're all here!"

"Yeah," I agree . . .

"This is the council chamber," Kevyn answers. "King Knothead and his advisers meet in this room."

"For what purpose?" Rovak asks.

Kevyn sneaks a glance at the formlings guarding our cell. "Before they invade, the bodkins intend to learn all they can about Byjovia and its people," he whispers. "They're looking for information."

FROM ME, THEY HOPE TO GAIN KNOWLEDGE OF BYJOVIAN HISTORY AND CUSTOMS!

FROM MILLIE, THEY MEAN TO DISCOVER THE SECRET WORKINGS OF MAGIC!

AND FROM SEDGEWICK, THEY SEEK TO LEARN METHODS OF COMBAT!

Simon frowns. "So they expect you to just spill the beans about whatever they ask?"

"**SURE**, I'LL TELL YOU ALL ABOUT BYJOVIA! HAVE FUN **CONQUERING** US!"

NO, THEY GIVE US **TRUTH SERUM!**

IT DOESN'T WORK, BUT WE **PRETEND** IT DOES!

WE'VE BEEN FEEDING THEM ALL KINDS OF NONSENSE!

WE TOLD THEM THAT "LOUIE LOUIE" IS THE BYJOVIAN NATIONAL ANTHEM!

...AND THAT KITTY LITTER IS A BREAKFAST CEREAL!

HA HA

"There's something I don't understand," Rovak interrupts. "You three are YOUNGSTERS. If the bodkins wanted to question people with EXPERIENCE..."

...WHY DIDN'T THEY KIDNAP **ADULTS?**

THEY CAN'T!

THE PORTAL WON'T **LET** THEM!

"The portal between Byjovia and Knot?" I say.

Kevyn nods. "Precisely."

The door opens with a creak and in walks a familiar figure. And another. And ANOTHER. A sick lump rises in my throat as I stare through the bars at King Knothead's council: the bodkins of Mumblin, Gadabout and Kevyn.

"So the reports are TRUE!" cackles the fake wizard. He sounds exactly like Mumblin. But there's no warmth.

The bogus Gadabout snickers. "From YOU, girl? Not a single thing."

UNLIKE YOUR LITTLE **FRIENDS**, YOU ARE OF NO **USE** TO US!

His words hang in the air like a putrid belch. He's right. Look who the bodkins chose to kidnap. Kevyn: smart. Millie: magical. Sedgewick: brave.

 AH! IT'S **TIME!**

BZZZZZZZZ

 SUMMON THE FORMLING!

YES, SIR!

IT'S TIME? TIME FOR WHAT?

I DON'T HAVE THE FAINTEST IDEA!

CURIOUS, ARE YOU?

FINE! I SHALL EXPLAIN THE PROCESS! THERE'S NOTHING YOU CAN DO TO STOP IT!

THE GODMOTHER WHO CREATED THIS WORLD—

DOGMOTHER.

✺AHEM!✺ THE **DOGMOTHER** DID NOT REALIZE...

...THAT SHE HAD UNKNOWINGLY FORGED A MAGICAL **BOND** BETWEEN **YOUR** WORLD AND **OURS!**

IN OTHER WORDS: WHENEVER A CHILD IS BORN IN BYJOVIA...

...A **BODKIN** EMERGES FROM THE PITS OF DOOM!

HISS SSSS

"So there really IS a bodkin for every man, woman and child in Byjovia?" I ask, a chill creeping down my back.

Fake Mumblin sneers. "Oh, yes."

ALL OF THEM EXIST AS VAPOROUS FORMLINGS FOR A **DECADE**...

...UNTIL THE TIME COMES FOR THEM TO *TRANSFORM!* WATCH CLOSELY!

THIS IS CALLED THE **CONNECTING STONE!**

IN IT, WE CAN OBSERVE IMPORTANT EVENTS AS THEY OCCUR IN BYJOVIA!

I SEE A GIRL!

WHAT'S IMPORTANT ABOUT **HER?**

IT'S THE CHILD'S **TENTH BIRTHDAY,** THAT'S WHAT!

"As the girl in Byjovia comes of age, so too does the formling!" fake Mumblin continues.

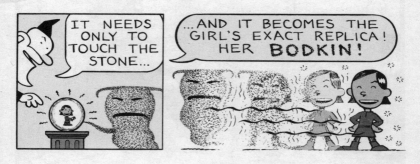

"Picture that happening dozens of times each week!" he chortles. "Thousands of times each year!"

THAT IS HOW WE'RE BUILDING AN ARMY!

"Byjovia has an army, too," Simon points out. "And it's a BIG one!"

"Shut your mouth, you wretched brat. Our side is well aware of your army," snarls Gadabout's bodkin.

Two formlings sweep into the room, and right behind them strides King Knothead. No surprise – he's a dead ringer for Conrad. Who did you THINK he'd look like? Uncle Budrick?

YOUR HIGHNESS, WE'VE CAPTURED THREE MORE PRISONERS.

GREAT SCOTT!

Knothead's eyes lock on to me. For a good ten seconds, his cold glare doesn't leave my face.

THAT GIRL. BRING HER HERE.

One of the formlings slithers between the iron bars. It yanks me up and out of the holding pen, tossing me to the floor like a piece of rubbish.

"I have seen you before," the king says as I struggle to my feet. "I watched you in the connecting stone."

YOU'RE THE GIRL WHO **SAVED BYJOVIA!**

Seems like a good time to play dumb.

"I don't know what you're talking about."

He smirks. "Then let me refresh your memory."

YOU STOOD BETWEEN KING CONRAD AND CERTAIN **DEATH**...

YOU SENT HIS BROTHER GASTLEY AWAY FOREVER...

AND YOU KILLED FENDRA, THE SORCERESS OF THE NORTH!

I keep my mouth clamped shut. What's there to say when an idiot like THIS guy pays you a compliment?

"I suppose I should thank you," Knothead goes on. "With Gastley and Fendra out of the way, MY path to the throne of Byjovia is much easier."

SHOOT HER? Not exactly what I was hoping to hear. There are shouts and cries from the other Midknights, but they sound miles away. The walls around me drift out of focus until all I see is the archer, calmly pulling an arrow from her quiver. She raises her bow, takes aim . . .

The shot hits me square in the heart and knocks me to the floor. I lie flat on my back, the twang of the bowstring still ringing in my ears.

Am I dead? No idea. I've never died before.

I open my eyes – that's a good sign, right? – and raise my head, fully expecting to see the arrow rising from my chest like a stalk of corn. But it isn't there.

HOW COULD THE ARROW STRIKE HER AND **BOUNCE OFF?**

"I – I cannot explain it, Your Highness," the archer stammers.

"TRY, you idiot!" Knothead barks. "See if she's hiding a suit of armour!" The archer kneels and grabs a fistful of my tunic.

"The girl wears only cloth," she reports.

I SEE NO WAY SHE COULD HAVE—

AH!

A look of surprise flits across her face, and I realize she's spotted the chain I'm wearing. With one violent yank, she pulls it from my neck. "HERE is the culprit!" she shouts.

A **GEMSTONE** WAS HIDDEN UNDER HER GARMENT!

THE ARROW POINT HIT THE GEM INSTEAD OF PIERCING HER HEART!

WHA–? GIVE IT HERE!

The crystal is lit up like a house on fire, because duh, we're knee-deep in evil. Knothead snatches the stone from the archer and stares at it with a mad gleam in his eyes.

Actually, HE didn't find it. The ARCHER did. But the guy's got a grade-A maniacal laugh going, so now's probably not the time to say anything.

THE REST OF YOU! SPREAD THE WORD!

HAVE EVERY BODKIN GATHER AT THE PORTAL!

YES, MY KING!

TELL THEM BYJOVIA WILL SOON BE OURS!

Knothead mounts the formling like it's a demon horse – even though, honestly, it looks more like a giant slug – and rushes from the room. Only the archer stays behind.

MY KING!

WAIT!

ARGH! HE DIDN'T TELL ME WHAT TO DO WITH THE **PRISONERS!**

I'M PRETTY SURE THE PRISONERS CAN TAKE CARE OF THEMSELVES!

HOORAY! THREE CHAIRS FOR MAX!

THREE **CHAIRS!** *CHUCKLE!* HOW DROLL!

MAX! GET US OUT OF HERE!

I dig through the archer's pockets and find a key to the cage. Seconds later, I've freed all the others. But there's no time for hugs and giggles.

"Did you hear that, guys?" I ask them. "Knothead thinks he's found a way to Byjovia!"

"Yes, and that crystal will apparently play a critical role in his plan," Kevyn says.

WHAT KIND OF ROLE?

I DON'T KNOW...

...BUT **SHE** MIGHT!

Kevyn scurries across the room, where a small vial of clear liquid rests on the council table.

WHAT'S THAT?

THE **TRUTH SERUM** THEY USED ON US!

BUT YOU SAID THAT STUFF DIDN'T **WORK!**

IT **DOESN'T...** ON **HUMANS!**

...BUT PERHAPS IT WILL WORK ON **BODKINS!**

Kevyn tips a few drops into the archer's mouth, and bingo – her eyes fly open. She's awake, in a just-got-hit-in-the-head-with-a-chair kind of way.

"I'm going to ask you some questions," Kevyn tells her.

"Ask, then." The archer's voice is lifeless.

WHY IS KING KNOTHEAD GOING TO THE PORTAL?

TO PASS THROUGH IT, OF COURSE...

...AND TO LEAD THE BODKINS TO BYJOVIA.

"But the portal works only for the young and the small," Kevyn points out.

"That will change," the archer croaks, "once the missing piece is restored to its proper place."

WHERE **IS** ITS PROPER PLACE?

YES, PLEASE EXPLAIN.

TELL US THE STORY OF THE MISSING PIECE!

We lean in as the archer begins her tale.

IT WAS A DARK AND STORMY NIGHT...

WHAT A CHEESY OPENING LINE.

SHH!

IN THE DAYS BEFORE KNOTHEAD BECAME KING...

...THE CROWN BELONGED TO THE VERY FIRST BODKIN: BORIS.

BORIS?

"He's the reason Knot was created in the first place!" I cry.

The archer nods. "Yes. He had become an old man."

BORIS HAD SPENT YEARS LOOKING FOR A WAY BACK TO BYJOVIA — TO SEEK REVENGE FOR HIS BANISHMENT.

GRRR

FINALLY, HE SUCCEEDED. IN THE PITS OF DOOM, HE FASHIONED A MAGICAL MIRROR...

...AND INSTALLED IT IN THE VERY CENTRE OF KNOT!

THIS WILL BE A PORTAL TO THE HUMAN WORLD!

HE RALLIED AN ARMY TO HIS SIDE.

BODKINS!! FOLLOW ME TO BYJOVIA!!

AS A STORM RAGED, BORIS STEPPED INTO THE MIRROR.

HA! IT'S WORKING!

BUT BEFORE HE FULLY VANISHED...

KR AK

...A BOLT OF LIGHTNING SHATTERED THE MIRROR INTO THOUSANDS OF CRYSTALS!

KSS SCH!

"AHA!" Kevyn yelps. "That closed the portal!"

"Correct," the archer confirms. "And Boris was killed. Knothead replaced him as king of the bodkins."

...AND JUST LIKE BORIS, KNOTHEAD BECAME OBSESSED WITH OPENING A PORTAL TO BYJOVIA.

HE ORDERED ALL THE SHARDS TO BE COLLECTED.

THEN, PAINSTAKINGLY, HE PIECED THE MIRROR BACK TOGETHER... ONLY TO MAKE A CRUCIAL DISCOVERY.

ONE TINY FRAGMENT WAS **MISSING**!

WITHOUT IT, THE PORTAL FUNCTIONED DIFFERENTLY. **SMALL** BEINGS COULD PASS THROUGH...

...BUT **LARGE** ONES COULD NOT!

WUMP!

AND SO THE ADULT BODKINS REMAINED TRAPPED IN KNOT.

"Until NOW," I groan, barely able to spit out the words. "What a chump I am!"

I JUST HANDED KNOTHEAD THE KEY TO BYJOVIA!

DON'T BLAME YOURSELF, MAX!

YEAH!

SHOVE

HOW WERE **YOU** SUPPOSED TO KNOW KNOTHEAD WAS LOOKING FOR **YOUR** CRYSTAL?

I get what they're saying – but none of it changes the fact that Knothead's on the move.

"We may not HAVE to go on foot," Rovak says, motioning us over to the window.

YIKES.

DEFINITELY NOT A CANDIDATE FOR THE "CUTEST PET" AWARD.

WHAT **IS** THAT, ROVAK?

A **CLATTERBACK**!

IT'S A COMBINATION OF MANY ANIMALS: TIGER, ALLIGATOR, SQUIRREL...

SQUIRREL?

GADZOOKS! IT'S A **MENAGERIE ON LEGS**!

AND TWO OF THOSE LEGS HAVE **HOOVES**! IT'S PART **HORSE**!

THAT MEANS IT CAN BE **TAMED**!

We race out of the castle and across the fields. The rest of us hang back as Simon approaches the creature.

NIIIICE CLATTERBACK... WANT A CARROT?

SNORT!

HOOOOO

I GUESS HE DOESN'T LIKE RAW VEGETABLES.

APPARENTLY, THIS BEAST IS ALSO PART **DRAGON**.

LOOK! IT'S LETTING SIMON **RIDE** IT!

BE CAREFUL, SIMON!

NO WORRIES, GUYS! IT'S GENTLE AS A **KITTEN!**

URK!

YAAAH!

STOMP! STOMP!

Some kitten. The clatterback rages across the fields, bucking like mad. There's no way Simon's ever ridden anything THIS wild. But after several frantic minutes ...

We scramble up on to the beast's back, Simon points it towards the centre of Knot ...

Famous last words. Two seconds later, the clatterback skids to a sudden stop. How sudden?

SPLURCH!

Yuck. Just what we DIDN'T need: a pool party in a giant mudhole. I try to paddle towards dry ground, but I can't move my legs. I feel myself sliding deeper into the muck, and with a sick rush it dawns on me: this isn't mud.

I squint up into the dust-grey sky. Dozens of tiny specks are circling above the treetops, drawing closer with each spiral. Yup, those are vultures.

A surge of anger rushes through me. We're just five kids and a dwarf trying to do the right thing – like KNIGHTS. Now we're about to get pecked to death by a flock of sky rats. Is that fair?

I'm shouting so loud, I almost don't hear it: a voice rising above the beating of wings and the sucking slurps of the quicksand. A voice I know better than anyone's.

Have you ever seen a person's head – like your uncle's, for instance – on the body of a giant bird of prey? Well, take it from me: it's completely bonkers.

And Budrick's not the only one getting his vulture on. A rescue party of human-bird hybrids is lifting us out of the quicksand one by one.

I GUESS WE'RE MAKING THE REST OF THIS TRIP BY **AIR**!

INDEED WE ARE!

SEYMOUR!

WE MEET AGAIN, MAX!

THANKS FOR SAVING US! I THOUGHT WE WERE **DEAD MEAT**!

HEY, NO PROBLEMO! WE'RE **VULTURES!**

DEAD MEAT IS OUR **SPECIALITY!!**

GROSS.

WAIT, WEREN'T YOU AND THE DWARFS IN THE **FOOTHILLS**?

"Yes," Seymour confirms, "until every bodkin in the land started marching to the centre of Knot. The clumsy oafs overran all our hiding places!"

IT BECAME IMPOSSIBLE TO CONCEAL OURSELVES ON THE GROUND...

...SO WE TOOK TO THE **SKIES**!

WOW! THAT'S IMPRESSIVE MAGIC!

ER... SPEAKING OF MAGIC, MILLIE...THERE'S SOMETHING I NEED TO TELL YOU.

I LOST YOUR WAND.

I swallow hard and tell her the whole story. When I get to the part about Kevyn's bodkin snapping her wand in half, she nods as if she's not surprised.

"I could feel it when it happened," she says.

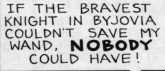

MAGICIANS AND THEIR WANDS HAVE A SUPER-CLOSE CONNECTION.

"I was supposed to keep it safe," I moan.

...AND I DIDN'T. I'M SORRY, MILLIE.

MAX, IT WASN'T YOUR FAULT!

IF THE BRAVEST KNIGHT IN BYJOVIA COULDN'T SAVE MY WAND, **NOBODY** COULD HAVE!

THE BRAVEST KNIGHT IN BYJOVIA? **ME?**

LOOK! WE'RE HERE!

WE'VE REACHED THE CENTRE OF KNOT!

We gaze down below. Thousands of bodkins are surging through the streets, all moving in the same direction.

"What if they see us?" Uncle Budrick squeaks.

"I don't think they will," Sedgewick counters.

THEY ONLY CARE ABOUT REACHING THE PORTAL!

I CONCUR!

LIKE BEES IN A HIVE, THEY'RE UNITED IN A COMMON MISSION!

HMM. **BEES**.

LET'S FIND A PLACE TO LAND... **QUICK**!

WE COULD TURN BACK INTO OURSELVES AT ANY—

POOF!

PIFF!

PUFF!

POFF!

YAAAAAAH!

SEYMOUR! CHANGE BACK!

THERE'S NO **TIME**!

BUT MAYBE **THIS** WILL DO THE TRICK!

STARS ALIGHT AND SUN ALOFT...

MAKE OUR LANDING PILLOW SOFT!

ZZZZ ZZAP!!

PLUFF!

PLOOMPF!

PLOOF!

PLUMPF!

WE'RE **ALIVE!**

WOW! SEYMOUR! YOU CREATED A CUSHION OF... OF...

WHAT **ARE** THESE? THEY SMELL **GOOD!**

FOR ABSOLUTELY NO REASON, I'M GOING TO CALL THEM MARSHMALLOWS!

THEY'W WEAWY THTICKY ON THE INTHIDE.

WOW, DID WE EVER LAND IN THE PERFECT SPOT!

YES, IN A PILE OF SUGARY **GOODNESS!**

NO, I MEAN WE'RE ON A **ROOFTOP!**

WE HAVE A CLEAR VIEW OF THE PORTAL FROM HERE!

LOOK! THERE'S KNOTHEAD!

Sure enough, the big jerk is standing before the roaring crowd. "Bodkins!" he shouts, calling them to attention.

AS YOU CAN SEE, THE MISSING PIECE OF THE MIRROR HAS BEEN **FOUND!**

THE PORTAL TO BYJOVIA HAS BEEN **REOPENED!**

For once, my timing's perfect. I drop silently to the street just as several heavy wagons roll past, piled high with iron and steel. It's a caravan of weapons from the forge.

Yeah, I know – ONE arrow. That's all I could grab. So sue me.

My heart sinks as Knothead disappears into the mirror. Other bodkins fall in line behind him. It's happening. He's on his way to Byjovia – and so is his army.

I take the rope from around my waist and tie it to the nock end of the arrow. Then . . .

Kevyn hands me a marshmallow and I split it open, exposing the gooey inner core. Then I fix it to the end of the arrow shaft. Let's hope it's sticky enough.

Sedgewick answers for me. "She can do this. She's the best shot in our class at KSB."

"Then I suggest you make haste, Max," Kevyn whispers. "Bodkins are entering the portal at an alarming rate."

They sure are – which is rough news for Byjovia. But as I pull back on the bowstring, I feel strangely calm. Sedgewick's right: I CAN do this. I take a deep breath and point the arrow straight at the crystal.

Then I let it fly.

GRAB THE ROPE, GUYS!

READY... SET... PULL!

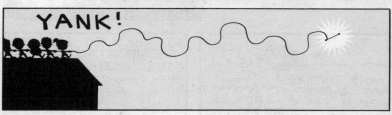

YANK!

IT **WORKED!** NOT ONLY DID THE ARROW COME BACK...

...IT BROUGHT THE CRYSTAL **WITH** IT!

BRILLIANT, MAX!

...AND IT WOULD APPEAR THAT YOUR SUPERB MARKSMANSHIP HAS HAD THE DESIRED EFFECT!

It's true. Down below, scores of angry bodkins are hurling themselves against the mirror. But without Queen Nerelia's crystal, there's nowhere to go. It's a dead end.

ZING!

...AND THEY'RE NOT HAPPY ABOUT IT!

THEY'VE **SEEN** US!

WE NEED TO GET TO THE PORTAL! IT'LL STILL WORK FOR **US**!

BUT IT'S SURROUNDED BY BODKINS!

THEY WON'T JUST STAND THERE AND LET US WALK THROUGH THE MIRROR!

"We won't HAVE to walk," I say.

SEYMOUR, IT'S TIME FOR **PLAN BEE**!

UH...WHAT'S THAT?

BZZ
BZZ
BZZ
BZZ
BZZ

AH! YES! GATHER AROUND, GANG!

"How?" Simon wonders. "WE shrank, but the crystal didn't! This thing's as big as a boulder!"

"Calm yourselves, Midknights!" Kevyn buzzes. "I assure you, the crystal is entirely portable!"

"I don't feel so good," the little wizard mumbles. "Casting so many spells has weakened me, I'm afraid."

"Climb on the crystal, Seymour!" I instruct him.

There's chaos up ahead. A gargantuan overbite keeps throwing a shoulder against the glass, trying to force his way through the portal. With every blow, a splintering crunch fills the air.

THE MIRROR IS **CRACKING**!

IF IT SHATTERS, WE'LL BE TRAPPED IN KNOT **FOREVER**!

I know what needs to be done – but I'm in no position to do it. I've got my hands (or legs, or whatever they are) full with Seymour and the crystal. I'm barely staying airborne.

Good thing there's another knight nearby.

BZZZZ

ROARR!

The surprised overbite staggers away from the mirror. It's still intact – but for how much longer?

"NOW, Midknights!" I shout.

12

You probably already know this, but I've never been a bee before. And flying head first into a magic mirror at full speed? That's a first, too.

It's not as fun as it sounds.

The portal's a much rougher ride this time. Picture a coal-black wind tunnel with teeth. It chews us up . . .

. . . and spits us out, sending us sprawling on to the grass. When I look around, I see that we're back in the Wandering Woods, under the same enormous tree. And that's not all.

"The roots and herbs that grow in Tresk have healing properties," Rovak explains. "If we take him there, he will soon regain his strength."

"Okay, Rovak, you're on," I tell him.

We shake hands. The dwarfs quickly fashion a makeshift stretcher for Seymour. As they carry him along the winding path that leads to Tresk, the rest of us set out for Byjovia as fast as we can.

We hike east through the forest, and it's rugged-going. There's no real path to follow – just some bent branches and flattened grass that tell us the bodkins have been here first.

We march for several hours.

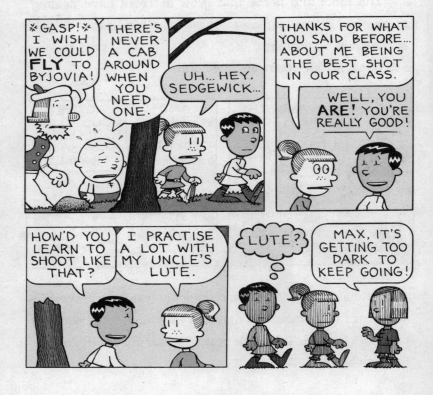

SHE'S RIGHT. I KEEP WALKING INTO TREES.

OKAY, LET'S CAMP HERE.

I'LL GO LOOK FOR FIREWOOD.

As we clear an area for sleeping, Sedgewick's words come back to me: YOU'RE REALLY GOOD. He didn't have to say that. But he did. That's got to mean something.

MAYBE I **DO** HAVE WHAT IT TAKES!

ARRGH!

THAT WAS **SIMON**!

We bolt towards the sounds of a struggle and find two boys grappling on the ground. One of them is Simon . . .

. . .AND SO'S THE **OTHER ONE**!

GRRR!

OOF!

Wow. Seeing the bodkins of people you know is strange enough. But watching Simon fight his OWN bodkin is totally bizarre.

The crystal! Why didn't I think of that? I fish it out of my pocket and wave it at the two Simons.

Hmm. This might be the world's shortest game of "Spot the Bodkin". I've just noticed something.

He's tongue-tied for a moment but recovers quickly. "Of COURSE I'm missing a tooth!" he splutters.

The bodkin's too quick for us. He darts into the shadows and disappears completely among the trees.

"Yeah, you'll get him next time, Simon," I say as we collect dry sticks for a fire.

"I hope so," he groans. "It's a lousy feeling, coming face to face with another ME."

"Sounds like it," I answer. "But I wouldn't know."

IF YOU WEREN'T BORN IN BYJOVIA, YOU **HAVE** NO BODKIN!

WELL, THAT'S SIMPLE ENOUGH! WHERE WERE YOU BORN, MAX?

I DON'T KNOW.

...AND NEITHER DO **YOU**, RIGHT, UNCLE BUDRICK?

VERY TRUE.

YOU COULD HAVE BEEN BORN **ANYWHERE** — INCLUDING THE LITTLE TOWN WHERE I FOUND YOU.

WAIT, YOU **FOUND** HER?

"Yes, indeed," Uncle Budrick begins. "I was a handsome young troubadour, travelling from hamlet to hamlet."

ONE DAY, I PUT ON A SHOW IN A VILLAGE CALLED GOBSMACK.

PLINKA PLINK PLONK

Budrick the JOLLY

THE CROWD **LOVED** IT!

SPLAT!

BOO!

YOU STINK!

AS I PREPARED TO BED DOWN FOR THE NIGHT, I HEARD A CRY...

WAAH!

...AND FOUND A **BABY** WRAPPED IN BLANKETS AND LEFT IN A CHURCH DOORWAY!

EGAD! MAX WAS THAT BABY!

YUP.

WHAT **ELSE** DO YOU REMEMBER?

JUST THAT SHE REALLY, REALLY NEEDED A NAPPY CHANGE.

ANDWEALL LIVEDHAPPILY EVERAFTER THEEND!

BLUSH!

BUT WHO LEFT YOU IN THE DOORWAY? WHO'S YOUR **FAMILY**?

UNCLE BUDRICK IS! AND **YOU GUYS** ARE!

WHAT MORE FAMILY DO I NEED?

GRAMMATICALLY INCORRECT, BUT NICELY SAID.

✵YAWN...✵ LET'S GET SOME REST, EVERYONE!

I stretch out on the grass, but it's hard to relax.

My thoughts turn to Byjovia. It could already be overrun with bodkins. Nerelia's crystal is on the fritz, and knowing who the bad guys are won't be easy. But I'll manage somehow.

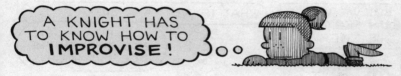

Uncle Budrick's still snoring louder than a wounded warthog. I scrape some moss from the ground and stuff it in my ears. Now that's improvising. Then I drift off into a good knight's sleep.

We're up bright and early the next morning with only one thing on our minds:

"We won't go LOOKING for a battle," Sedgewick points out.

After another hour of hiking, we reach Byjovia's outer walls. We bypass the main archway and enter through a side gate, only a few steps from the KSB training yard.

Sedgewick and I sprint to the armoury and push open the door. Inside, there's every sort of hardware imaginable.

We whirl round to see Sir Brickbat blocking the doorway like a giant boulder, a look of disgust on his face.

"First a bad student, and now a THIEF!" he roars. "Just what I'd expect from the likes of YOU, girlie!"

"I'm no thief," I tell him.

"She hasn't talked me into anything," Sedgewick says, gathering up an armful of blades.

Brickbat turns white with fury as we edge past him. "I'm going to assume, Sedgewick, that you will eventually come to your senses," he hisses. "But for YOU, girl, this is the last straw. You're officially expelled from this school!"

We race back to the others with Sir Brickbat's shouts of rage trailing after us.

"I quite agree," pants Kevyn as we dash through the maze of winding streets. "That knavish Knothead will undoubtedly attempt to replace Conrad!"

THEN IT'LL BE UP TO **US** TO SNIFF HIM OUT!

IF YOU NOTICE ANYTHING SKETCHY ABOUT KING CONRAD, **SAY** SOMETHING!

GREETINGS, MY DEAR CHAP!

THE **MIDKNIGHTS** REQUEST AN AUDIENCE WITH THE KING!

ALL RIGHT, THEN...

...BUT LEAVE YOUR WEAPONS HERE.

WHAT?

"But we're the king's FRIENDS!" I protest.

"So you say," the guard replies, collecting our blades.

...BUT WITH ALL DUE RESPECT, YOU MIGHT BE A **BODKIN**!

"I guess that makes sense," I say as we continue towards the throne room. "We don't know if King Conrad's a bodkin...

...AND HE DOESN'T KNOW IF **WE'RE** BODKINS!

WAIT, **ARE** WE BODKINS?

NO.

MAX!

WELCOME BACK! SO GOOD TO SEE YOU!

GADABOUT!

...AND **MILLIE!** YOU'RE **SAFE!**

YES, THANKS TO MAX AND THE MIDKNIGHTS!

Hmm. He SEEMS like the real Gadabout, but I've got to be sure. As he greets the others, I watch with eagle eyes for even the tiniest giveaway – like Sedgewick's freckle or Simon's missing tooth or . . .

He smiles kindly. "Believe me, Max. There's no need to explain. I understand completely."

"Know what's even MORE awful?" Uncle Budrick chirps.

I hesitate. "I don't know if I should."

There's that smile again. "Max, you can trust me! It's your old friend Gadabout!"

"But I can assure you, the bodkins are not a threat! King Conrad has seen to that!"

I relax a little. Maybe Byjovia doesn't need saving after all.

"Um . . . where IS King Conrad?" I ask.

"Here," a voice calls, and into the room steps a familiar figure, his eyes twinkling.

"Good day, Your Majesty," the other Midknights chime. But I say nothing. The king notices.

"Why so quiet, Max? Have you no greeting for your king?"

I take a deep breath. "Yes, I do."

13

The bodkin's face hardens into a scowl, and he fixes me with an icy stare.

"You're full of surprises, aren't you?" he snarls.

"The REAL Conrad hates those frilly clothes," I tell him. "He only wears them when he HAS to."

Knothead smirks. "Well spotted, girl. You seem rather bright – for a human."

Boy, do I wish I had a weapon. "I'd never join the likes of you!" I shout. "I'd rather DIE!"

Knothead reaches for a lever on the wall.

The floor disappears. We plunge straight down for one heart-stopping moment. Then...

GROAN... SINCE WHEN DOES THE THRONE ROOM HAVE A **TRAPDOOR**?

IT WAS INSTALLED BY MY FATHER, KING BENTLEY!

IT'S HOW HE DEALT WITH TRAVELLING SALESMEN!

CONRAD!

AND **YOU'RE** THE GENUINE GADABOUT!

INDEED! WELCOME TO THE DUNGEON, MY FRIENDS!

I WISH WE WERE MEETING UNDER HAPPIER CIRCUMSTANCES.

HOW'D YOU GUYS END UP HERE?

Gadabout grimaces. "We were taken by surprise. Last night I sent some of my men out on patrol . . ."

...AND WHEN THEY RETURNED TO THE CASTLE, SOMETHING SEEMED **ODD**.

AH-**HA**! THEY'D BEEN REPLACED BY **BODKINS**, CORRECT?

YES, BUT BY THE TIME WE REALIZED IT, WE'D BEEN CAPTURED.

BUMMER.

"I wasn't vigilant enough," Gadabout continues. "It was entirely my fault."

"YOUR fault?" I echo in surprise.

BUT YOU'RE A **KNIGHT**!

KNIGHTS DON'T MAKE MISTAKES!

...DO THEY?

OF COURSE! ALL THE TIME!

THERE'S NO SUCH THING AS A PERFECT KNIGHT!

WHAT HAPPENED TO YOUR MEN? WHERE ARE THEY NOW?

"They are locked away, just as we are," Gadabout answers.

THE ENTIRE DUNGEON IS FILLED WITH INNOCENT BYJOVIANS!

THANK GOODNESS **MUMBLIN** MANAGED TO ESCAPE!

HE **DID**? THAT'S **GREAT**!

CAN WE **CALL** HIM? DOES ANYONE HAVE SOME **FRUIT**?

NOPE.

ALL I HAVE IS THIS **TOMATO** SOMEONE THREW AT ME LAST WEEK.

BUDRICK! A TOMATO **IS** A FRUIT!

I THOUGHT IT WAS A VEGETABLE.

TRUST ME! I'VE READ "THE BIG BOOK OF BYJOVIAN BOTANY" **TEN TIMES**!

LET'S TRY IT!

"That shouldn't be a problem," Sedgewick says. "There are bodkins all over Byjovia."

"I'm . . . uh . . . not quite myself at the moment," Mumblin replies. "I don't even have my wand handy."

"You don't need a wand," I explain. "Remember when you hypnotized Uncle Budrick so he'd stop eating fried food?"

The guard's eyes light up. "Magic, you say? GIVE IT!"
I hand him the tomato through the bars.

YOU ARE VERY RELAXED.

I AM VERY RELAXED.

YOU WILL OBEY MY EVERY COMMAND.

I WILL OBEY YOUR EVERY COMMAND.

UNLOCK THE CELL.

'KAY.

SAVED BY A TOMATO!

WE'LL FREE THE OTHER PRISONERS, MAX, WHILE YOU DELIVER A BODKIN TO MUMBLIN!

I'VE GOT JUST THE BODKIN IN MIND!

First, though, I have to take a quick detour. I race to the checkpoint where we entered the castle.

HEY, CAN I HAVE MY DAGGER BACK?

NO.

YOUR WEAPON IS NOW THE PROPERTY OF—

KLONG!

SORRY ABOUT THIS...

...BUT WITH ALL DUE RESPECT, YOU MIGHT BE A **BODKIN!**

The corridor's empty – a lucky break for me. I make my way to the throne room and slip inside unnoticed.

THESE BYJOVIANS ARE SUCH GULLIBLE **FOOLS!**

THEY HAVE NO IDEA WE'RE NOT WHO WE **SAY** WE ARE!

HA HA

HA HA HA HA HA HA

HA HA HA

"That's why this plan will work!" Knothead snickers. "When I give my speech, all the people will attend . . ."

...AND THEY'LL BE SO CONVINCED I'M THEIR **KING**, THEY'LL DO WHATEVER I **TELL** THEM TO!

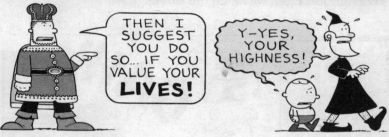

The two bodkins split up after scurrying out of the throne room, and I quietly fall in behind fake Kevyn. I wait until we're well clear of the doorway, and then . . .

The threat works. Never mind that the only chopping I've ever done was making coleslaw for the KSB potluck.

As we leave the castle grounds, I tuck the dagger up my sleeve. No sense calling attention to ourselves. Blending in with the crowd, I nudge fake Kevyn through the busy streets. Five minutes later, we reach the stable.

"Please, Max," Mumblin says. "Take a spoonful from the cauldron and splash it on me!"

Fake Kevyn begins to twitch and shake. His hair changes colour, and then his skin and clothing do the same until his whole body is an ashy grey. His arms and legs wither and fade into a blur.

With an ear-splitting screech, the formling rockets out of the stable and into the sky as if launched from a catapult.

"It identified him as a bodkin and also restored him to his original form!" Mumblin declares. "Then, for good measure, it sent him away! Back to Knot, no doubt!"

OUR AIR IS TOO CLEAN AND OUR SUN IS TOO BRIGHT FOR FORMLINGS TO SURVIVE IN **OUR** WORLD!

IF ONLY WE COULD TARGET **ALL** THE BODKINS WITH THE POTION AT THE SAME TIME!

MAYBE WE **CAN**! FAKE CONRAD IS MAKING A **SPEECH** TODAY!

THE WHOLE **KINGDOM** WILL BE THERE! BYJOVIANS **AND** BODKINS!

AH-**HA**! SO ALL WE NEED TO DO IS MAKE IT RAIN **POTION** INSTEAD OF **WATER**!

SOUNDS EASY ENOUGH.

"We can do it!" Mumblin claims. "First, though, I must make myself WHOLE again!"

IN MY BAG YOU'LL FIND SOME PILLS, MAX. BRING THEM TO ME, PLEASE.

OKAY.

"Pop one into my mouth," he instructs me.

"And now let's proceed with our plan!" Mumblin announces as he cleans out nostril number two. "I'm going to change the composition of the potion from liquid . . ."

"You'll understand soon enough!" he says, scooping the seeds from the cauldron into a burlap sack.

Mumblin steers us into a steep climb, through a thick bank of clouds, and into the clear skies above.

"Max, grab your dagger," Mumblin instructs me.

I do as he says, poking my blade through the burlap. Seeds pour from the hole and settle into the clouds below us.

"All clouds are made of water," Mumblin explains. "Our seeds will mix with that water . . ."

When the sack is empty, we circle down to the ground, landing in the paddock beside the stable.

"The rain should start in about an hour," Mumblin predicts.

"Perfect timing," I say. "Knothead will be right in the middle of his speech by then!"

The old wizard winks. "Excellent."

It's Fake Mumblin, rushing towards us with an evil grin creasing his face. The real Mumblin is unimpressed.

"That looks like one of my old wands," he observes.

"It WAS!" the bodkin corrects him . . .

"Poor chap," Mumblin mutters after a long silence.

"POOR CHAP?!" I repeat in disbelief.

"He messed up, huh?"

Mumblin smiles. "It seems his plan didn't go as expected."

I gaze at the darkening clouds overhead and the throngs of people streaming towards the square. "I hope OUR plan goes as expected."

14

"What time do you think it is?" I ask Mumblin after a while.

"Allow me to consult my latest invention!" he chuckles, rolling up his sleeve.

I CALL IT...A **WRISTWATCH!**

SQUAWK!

UH... THAT'S A BIRD STRAPPED TO YOUR ARM.

TRUE! BUT HE KNOWS THE TIME! LISTEN!

SQUAWK! IT'S EXACTLY 2:55 P.M.!

SEE?

2:55? KNOTHEAD'S **SPEECH** IS ABOUT TO START!

RRRUMBLE!

AND SO IS OUR **POTION STORM**! COME, MAX! LET'S GET TO THE SQUARE!

WOW!

"It's a total MOB SCENE!" I exclaim.

Mumblin nods. "And look how happy the people seem. None of them suspect that there are bodkins among them."

The crowd breaks into a tremendous roar. Fake Conrad has just emerged from the castle.

"I'm going to move closer to the stage," Mumblin tells me.

In other words: if I find people inside a building or under a roof, I'll move 'em into the open.

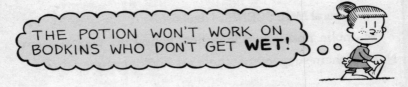

THE POTION WON'T WORK ON BODKINS WHO DON'T GET **WET!**

There's a trumpet blast, and the audience falls silent. The bogus king raises a hand in greeting. "Welcome, my fellow Byjovians!" he proclaims.

...AND **THANK YOU** FOR JOINING ME HERE TODAY!

YAAAY!

I gotta hand it to the guy: he makes a mighty convincing Conrad. And the people are eating it up.

THEY'RE GONNA **FLIP** WHEN THEY REALIZE THEY'VE BEEN CHEERING FOR HIS—

...EVIL TWIN!

So here she is at last: my bodkin. But this isn't the way I pictured it. I thought we'd meet face to face . . .

She ushers me through a doorway and into a vacant shopfront. It's not a big space . . .

"So I see," she mutters. She points her dagger at my chest and glares at me, her eyes blazing.

WHO ARE YOU?

Really? After so much drama, THAT'S her question?

"You obviously know who I am," I growl, "since all you are is a COPY of me!"

She looks outraged. "ME a copy?"

YOU'RE THE—

KABOOM!

From outside comes an ear-splitting clap that's so loud, we both drop our daggers. That was no ordinary thunder. We exchange a glance and instantly we have the same thought: fighting can wait.

TRUCE.

...FOR **NOW!**

We dash to the window. Dark clouds hang low over the square, but there's no rain yet. My eyes move to the platform, where Knothead continues to speak.

"Let us consider the question of loyalty," he proclaims. "Do you understand the word?"

"It is no trick," the real Conrad assures the crowd.

Above the buzz of confusion rising from the square, Knothead struggles to be heard. "These are the words of a babbling fool!" he shouts. "Pay no mind to this buffoon!"

He lunges at the king. But just then there's another roll of thunder, and raindrops begin to pour from the sky. FINALLY.

The crowd screeches in fear. "What's happening?" one woman wails.

It's just like seeing bogus Kevyn change into a formling – only this time, ALL the bodkins are doing it.

"Are you kidding?" she snaps. "Why would I do that?"

Good point. I should have known she'd need some convincing. Looks like we're doing this the hard way.

We duel. She's a good fighter, but she hasn't practised against the best like I have. Using a few Sedgewick-like moves, I'm able to force her out of the door . . . and into the rain.

I wait for her skin to change colour. For her arms and legs to wither away. For her body to transform into a shadowy mass of grey smoke.

It doesn't happen.

Ouch. A flying elbow sends me tumbling to the ground. Not exactly my knightliest moment. I'm face down in the street . . .

...WHEN I **SHOULD** BE FIGHTING MY **BODKIN!**

WHERE'D SHE GO?

MAX! **THERE** YOU ARE!

MILLIE!

ER...YOU **ARE** MILLIE, AREN'T YOU?

SHE MOST ASSUREDLY **IS!**

HER BODKIN — IN FACT, **ALL** THE BODKINS — HAVE BEEN **VANQUISHED!**

LET'S KEEP IT THAT WAY!

MUMBLIN, PROCEED TO THE WANDERING WOODS AND CLOSE THE PORTAL TO KNOT **PERMANENTLY**.

YES, YOUR MAJESTY!

"Yours?" Sedgewick asks. "Where is she?"

I feel my cheeks grow warm. "Umm . . . she got away," I admit.

BUT SHE WAS **RIGHT HERE!** AND THE POTION DIDN'T AFFECT HER **AT ALL!**

"How can that be?" Uncle Budrick wonders. "Mumblin said the potion was FOOLPROOF!"

"There can be only one explanation," Kevyn concludes.

There's an awkward silence. Conrad and Gadabout exchange some whispered words. Then the old knight clears his throat.

"Max, do you remember when I left knight school?"

SURE. KING CONRAD SENT YOU ON SOME KIND OF MISSION.

YES.

I WAS TO LEARN WHATEVER I COULD ABOUT **THIS** PERSON.

From a small pouch he pulls a battered golden locket and pries it open. Inside rests a tiny painted portrait.

IT'S **ME**!

BUT THAT'S **IMPOSSIBLE**! I'VE NEVER POSED FOR A PAINTING!

"Look at the other side," Gadabout says gently.

He tips the locket into his palm, and the portrait drops out. On the plain wooden backing is etched a name.

MARY

MARY? WHO THE HECK IS **MARY**?

AFTER TODAY'S EVENTS, I THINK WE KNOW!

SHE'S THE YOUNG LADY YOU JUST MET AND MISTOOK FOR A **BODKIN!**

SO MY BODKIN IS... JUST A **GIRL?**

MORE THAN JUST A GIRL, MAX. **MUCH** MORE.

As Gadabout's words sink in, my whole body starts to tingle. I understand now. Thanks to that tiny portrait, I'm finally seeing the big picture.

MARY'S... MY **SISTER,** ISN'T SHE?

MY **TWIN** SISTER!

Gadabout smiles. "It's rather exciting news!"

"Well . . . yeah, maybe," I mumble. "If she's nice."

I turn around, and there's Uncle Budrick. I forget sometimes what a kind face he has. But I notice it now.

"I'm happy for you, Max," he says, his voice cracking.

"Only if you're a part of it," I tell him. "We stick together."

Uncle Budrick peels off towards the castle with Conrad and Gadabout. Mumblin reunites with Seymour and leaves for the Wandering Woods. I join the rest of the Midknights and head for . . . well, I'm not really sure.

"Where should we start?" I ask. As usual, Kevyn's happy to provide an answer.

"Before we embark on our NEXT adventure, I must write about THIS one!" he announces. "The tale of those despicable creatures from Knot will make a stupendous book!"

"What's it gonna be called?" Simon asks.

"BATTLE OF THE BODKINS!" Kevyn replies. "And I already know how it ends!"

...WITH OUR HEROES WALKING OFF INTO THE SUNSET!

end

Don't miss Max & the Midknights' epic beginning!
Read the instant *New York Times* bestseller now!

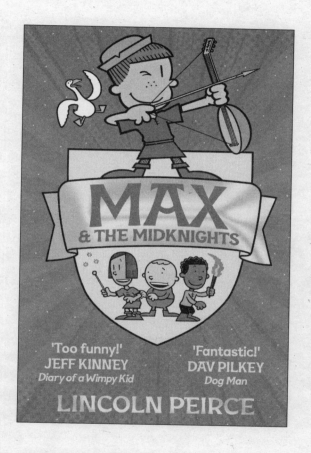

"Pure fun." —The New York Times

"A knight's tale in shining armor."
—Kirkus Reviews

I'm going to tell you a secret: being a troubadour kind of stinks.

You know what troubadours are, right? They're travelling entertainers. And it's actually my uncle Budrick who's the troubadour, not me. He does all the singing and juggling. I'm just along for the ride.

You could call me his apprentice, I guess. I'm supposed to practise the lute (the instrument he's playing that looks like a giant chicken leg), learn all the songs, and prepare myself just in case Uncle Budrick sprains a tonsil. But here's the problem:

Why not? Well, you're on the road all the time, for one thing. That's a total drag. It's hard to make friends, too, because you're always moving from village to village. And this wagon we live in isn't exactly a four-star hotel. What else? Oh, yeah . . .

It's the MIDDLE AGES!

Yup, we're talking fourteenth century. That means a lot of important stuff hasn't been invented yet. Like paved roads, the toothbrush, and a little convenience known as indoor plumbing. It's a tough life, and – sorry, Uncle Budrick – I can't see how a few songs or some lame magic tricks will make it any easier.

About the Author

Lincoln Peirce is a *New York Times* bestselling author and cartoonist. His comic strip Big Nate, featuring the adventures of an irrepressible sixth grader, appears in over 400 newspapers worldwide and online. In 2010 he began a series of illustrated novels based on the strip, which have sold over sixteen million copies.

Max and the Midknights originated as a proposed TV series set in the Middle Ages. Lincoln later rewrote the story – which includes hundreds of dynamic illustrations in his trademark style – as a medieval adventure centred around Max, a ten-year-old who dreams of becoming a knight.

When he is not writing or drawing, Lincoln enjoys playing ice hockey, doing crossword puzzles, and hosting a weekly radio show devoted to vintage country music. He and his wife, Jessica, have two children and live in Portland, Maine.